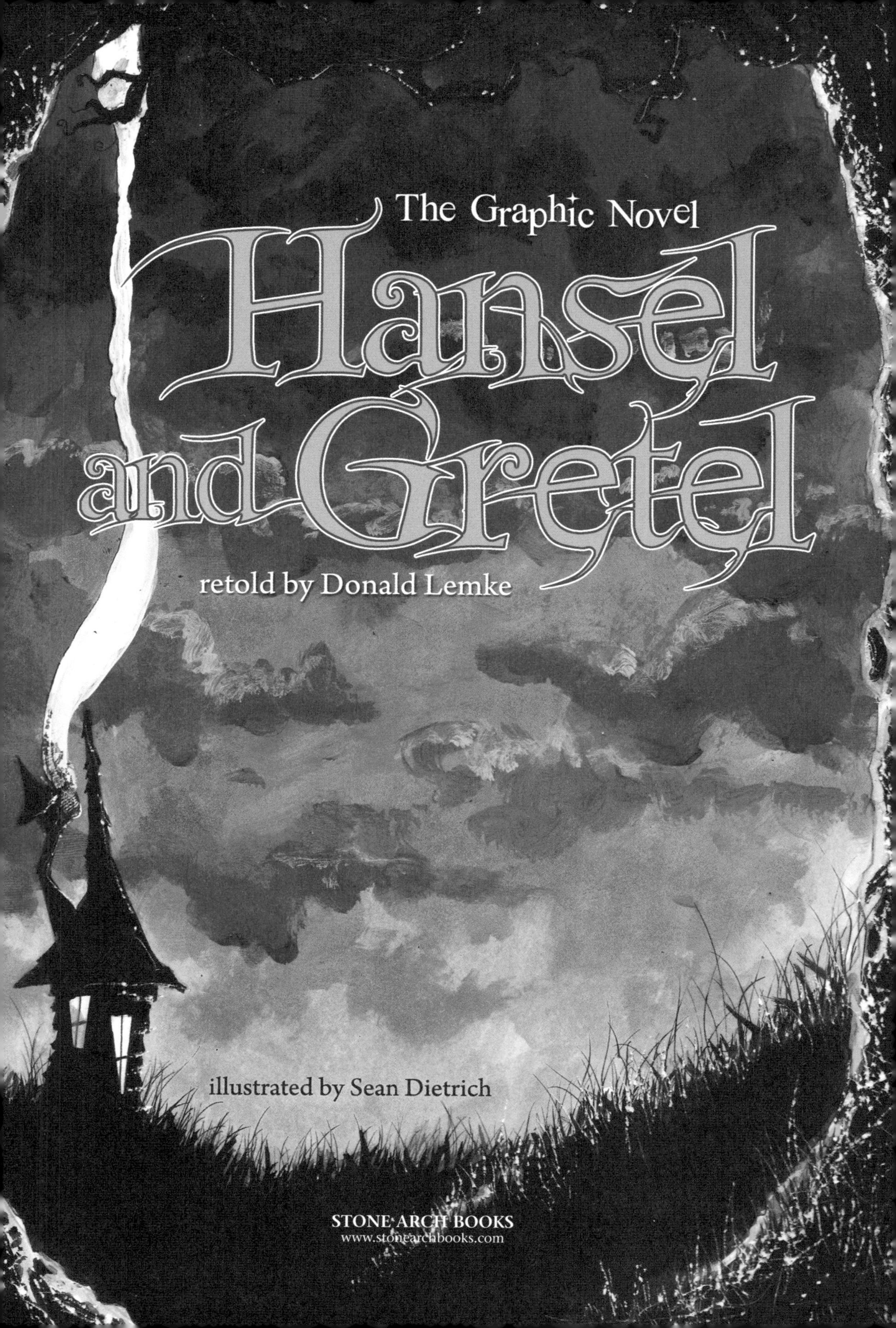

The Graphic Novel

Hansel and Gretel

retold by Donald Lemke

illustrated by Sean Dietrich

STONE ARCH BOOKS
www.stonearchbooks.com

Graphic Spin is published by Stone Arch Books
151 Good Counsel Drive, P.O. Box 669
Mankato, Minnesota 56002
www.stonearchbooks.com

Copyright © 2009 by Stone Arch Books

All rights reserved. No part of this publication may be reproduced
in whole or in part, or stored in a retrieval system, or transmitted in any
form or by any means, electronic, mechanical, photocopying, recording,
or otherwise, without written permission of the publisher.

Library of Congress Cataloging-in-Publication Data
Lemke, Donald B.
   Hansel and Gretel: The Graphic Novel / retold by Donald Lemke; illustrated by Sean Dietrich.
   p. cm. — (Graphic Spin)
   ISBN 978-1-4342-0767-8 (library binding)
   ISBN 978-1-4342-0863-7 (pbk.)
   1. Graphic novels. [1. Graphic novels.] I. Dietrich, Sean, ill. II. Hansel and Gretel. English.
III. Title.
PZ7.7.L46Han 2009
741.5'973—dc22   2008006721

Summary: When their parents leave them in the forest, Hansel and Gretel must find their way home.
During their journey, they discover something better — a house made of sugary sweets! Too bad it's
owned by an evil, and hungry, old witch.

Art Director: Heather Kindseth
Graphic Designer: Kay Fraser / Brann Garvey

Librarian Reviewer
Katharine Kan
Graphic novel reviewer and Library Consultant, Panama City, FL
MLS in Library and Information Studies, University of Hawaii at Manoa, HI

Reading Consultant
Elizabeth Stedem
Educator/Consultant, Colorado Springs, CO
MA in Elementary Education, University of Denver, CO

1 2 3 4 5 6 13 12 11 10 09 08

Printed in the United States of America

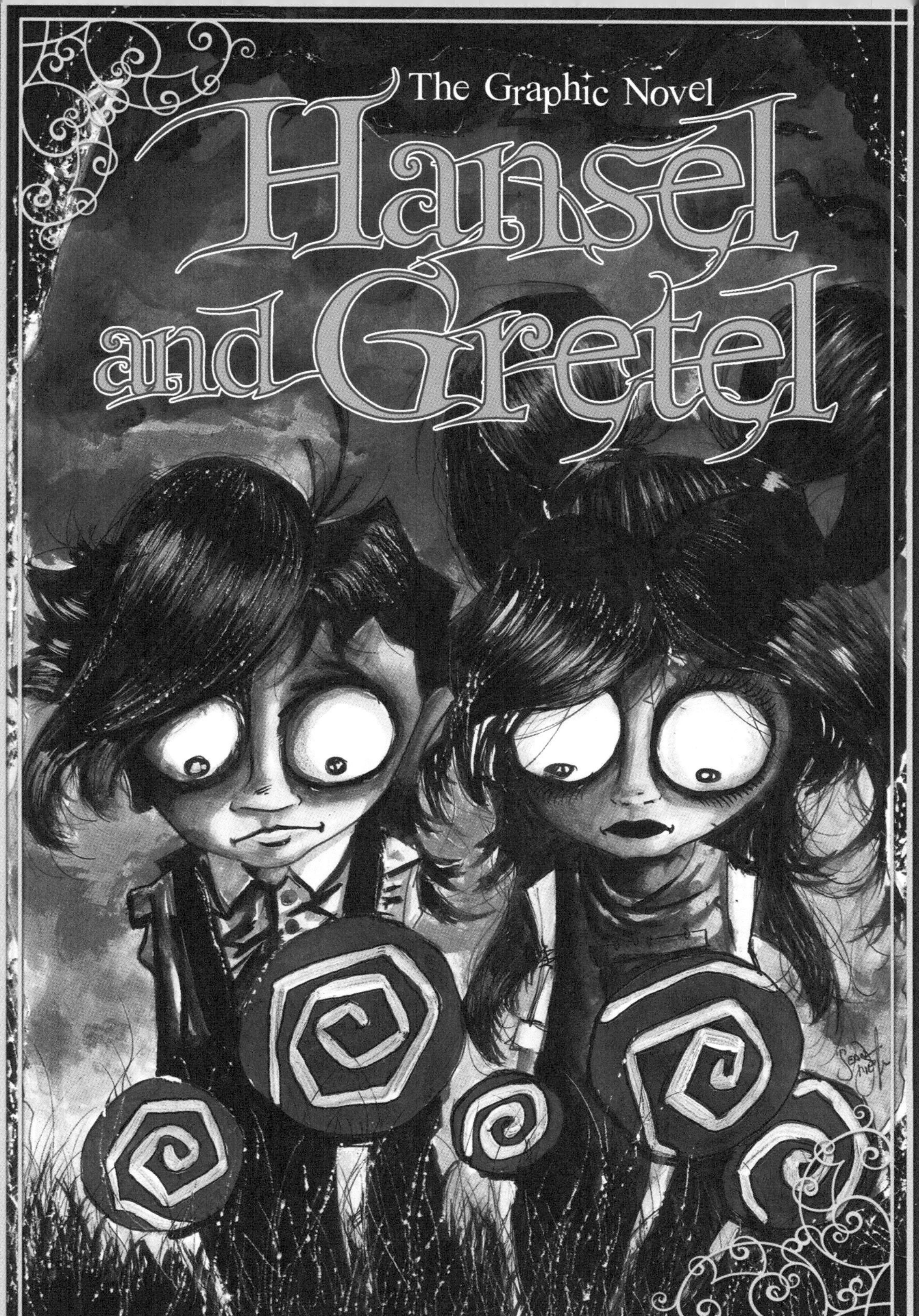
The Graphic Novel
Hansel and Gretel

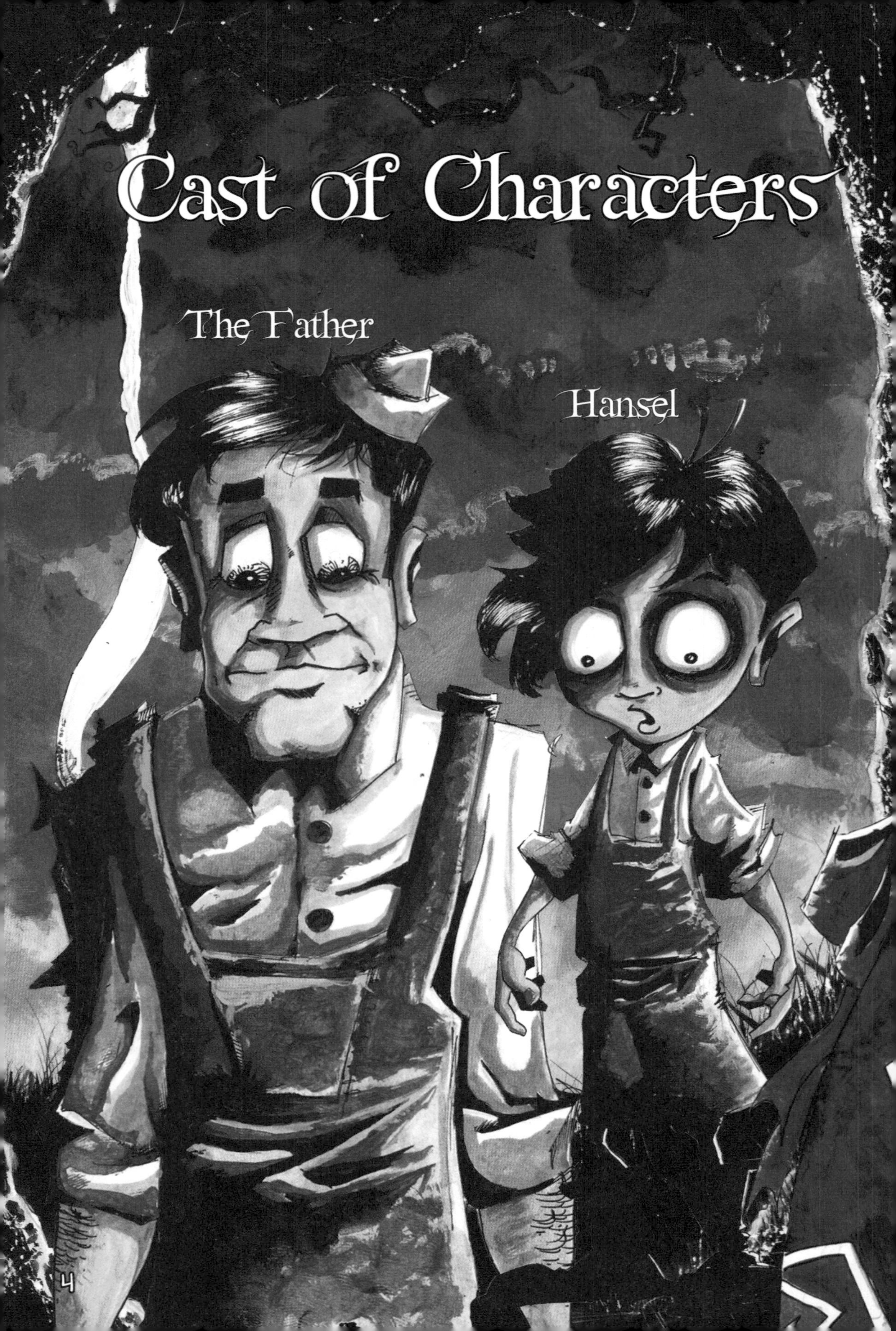
Cast of Characters
The Father
Hansel

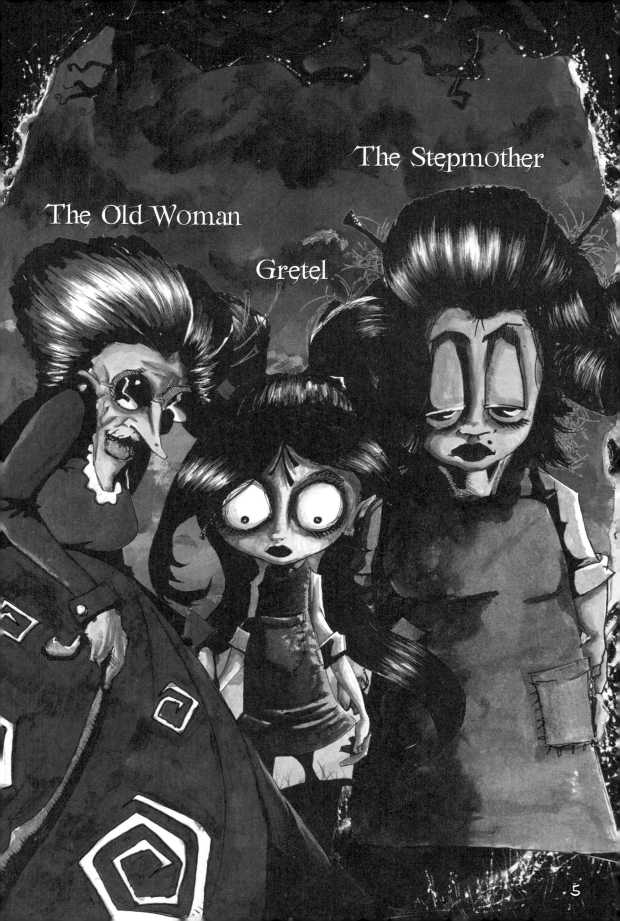

The Old Woman

The Stepmother

Gretel

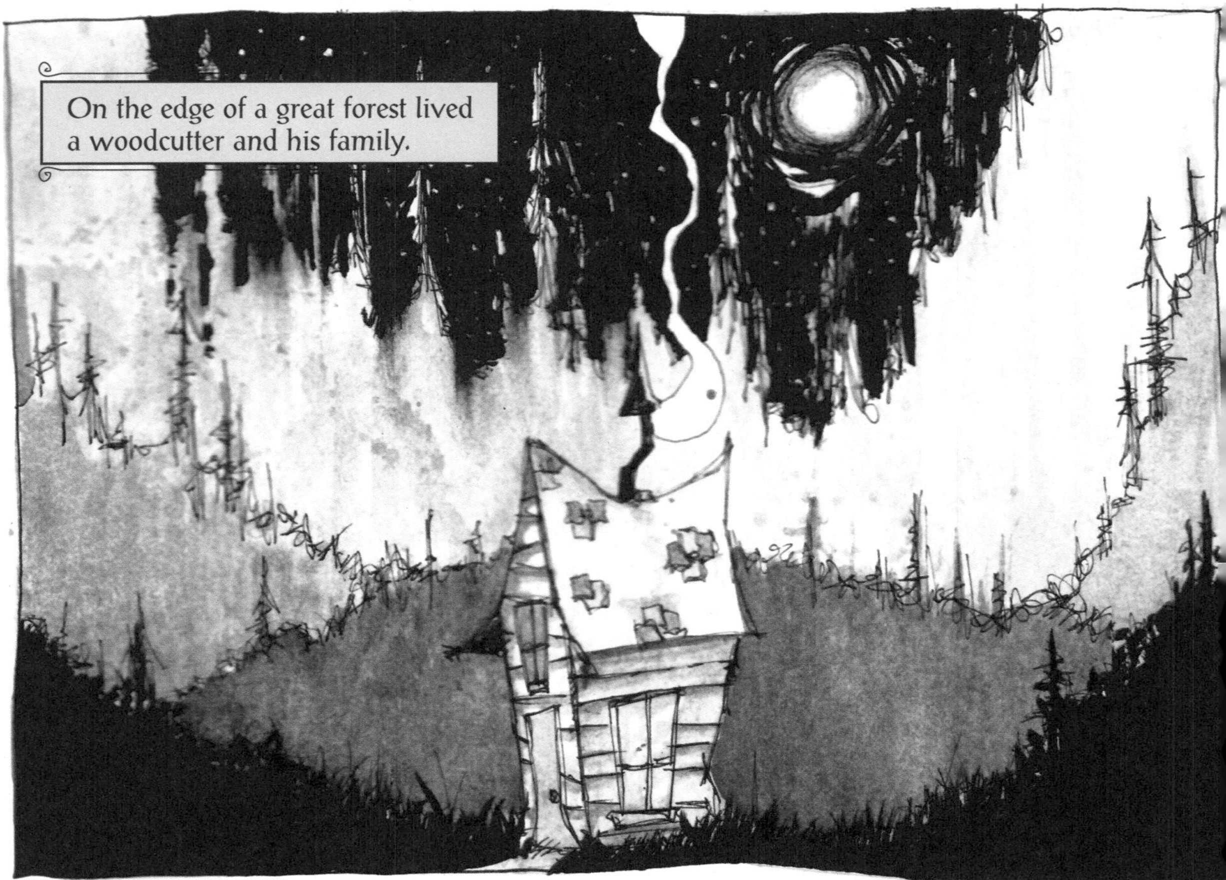
On the edge of a great forest lived a woodcutter and his family.

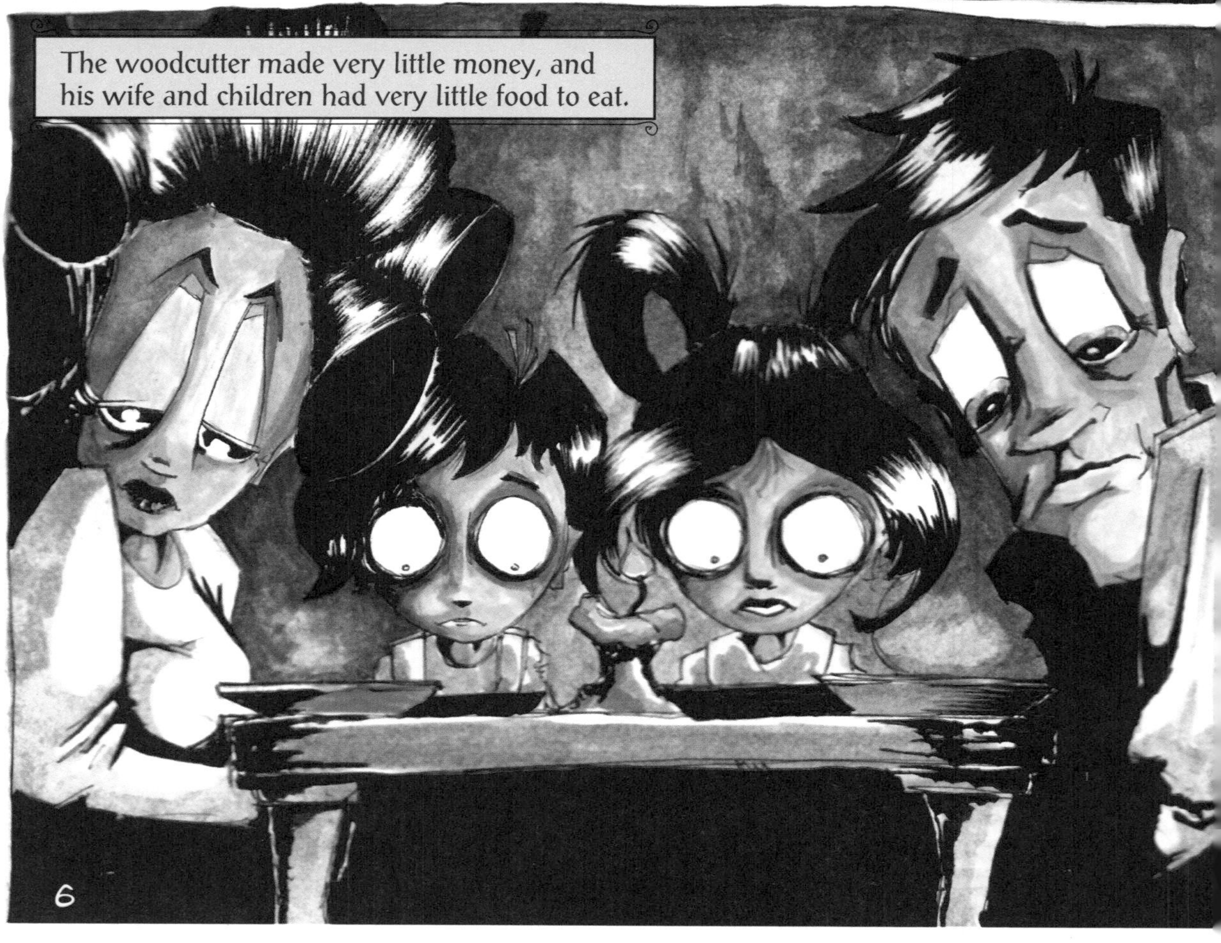
The woodcutter made very little money, and his wife and children had very little food to eat.

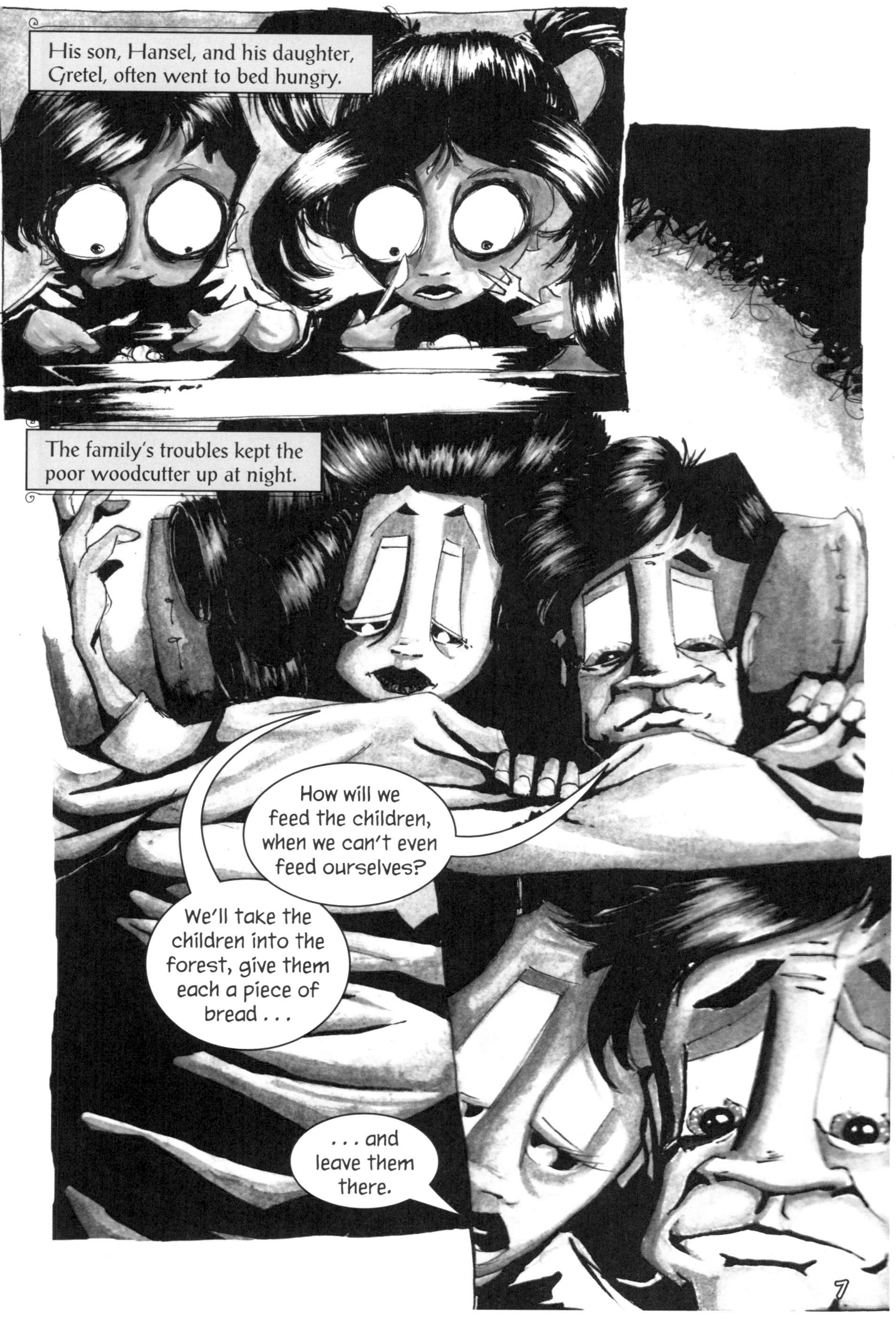
His son, Hansel, and his daughter, Gretel, often went to bed hungry.
The family's troubles kept the poor woodcutter up at night.
How will we feed the children, when we can't even feed ourselves?
We'll take the children into the forest, give them each a piece of bread . . .
. . . and leave them there.

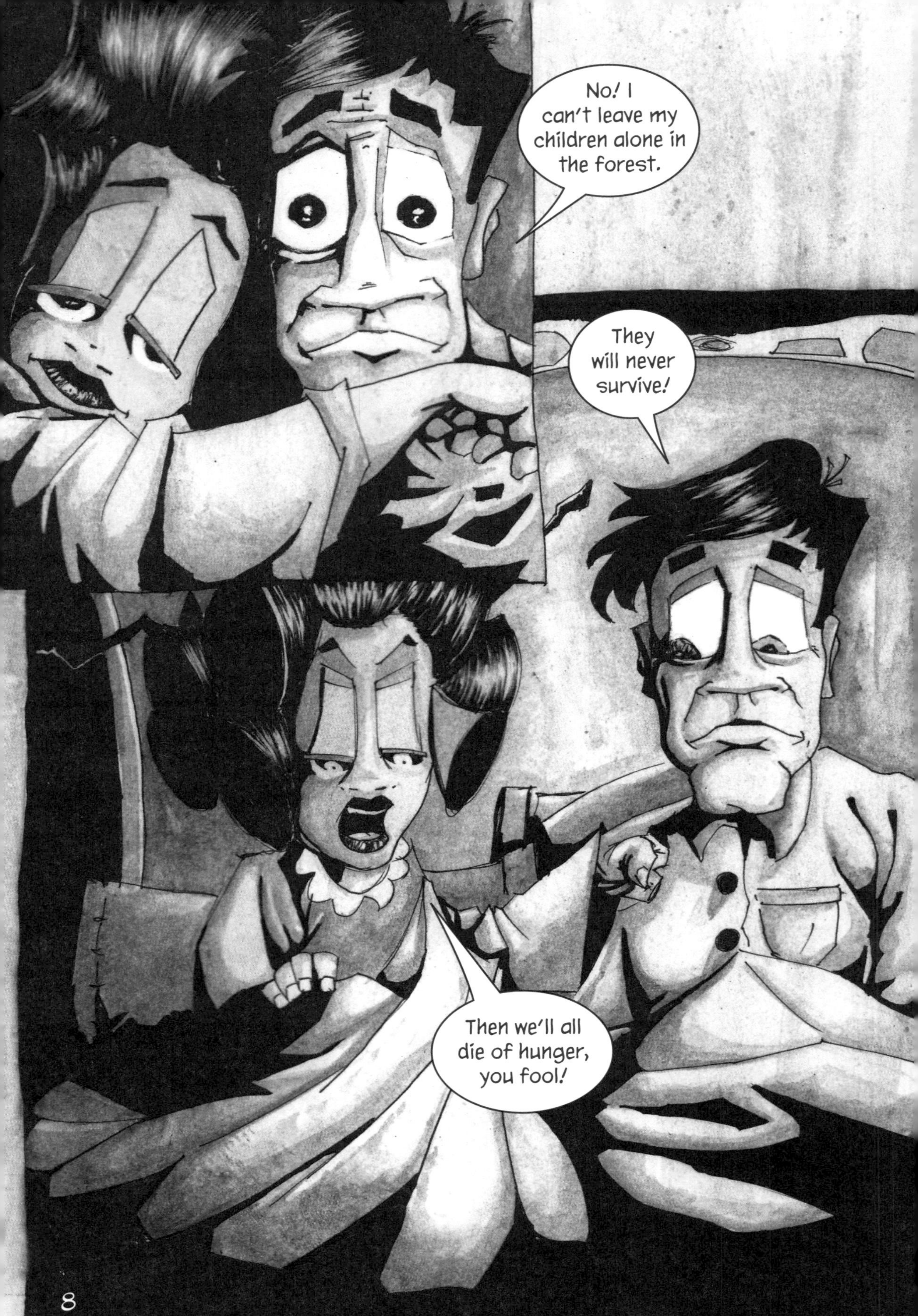
No! I can't leave my children alone in the forest.
They will never survive!
Then we'll all die of hunger, you fool!

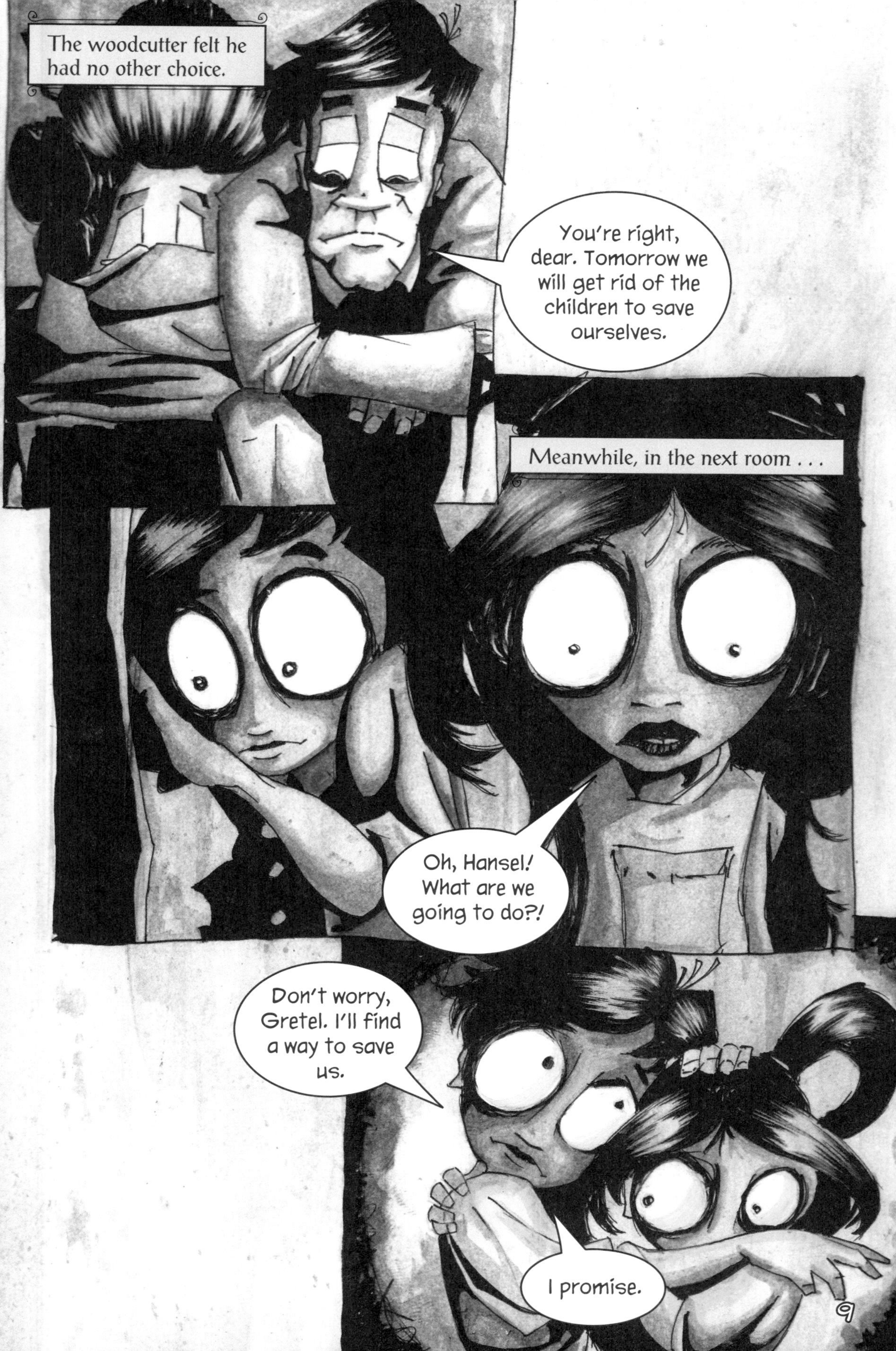
The woodcutter felt he had no other choice.
You're right, dear. Tomorrow we will get rid of the children to save ourselves.
Meanwhile, in the next room . . .
Oh, Hansel! What are we going to do?!
Don't worry, Gretel. I'll find a way to save us.
I promise.

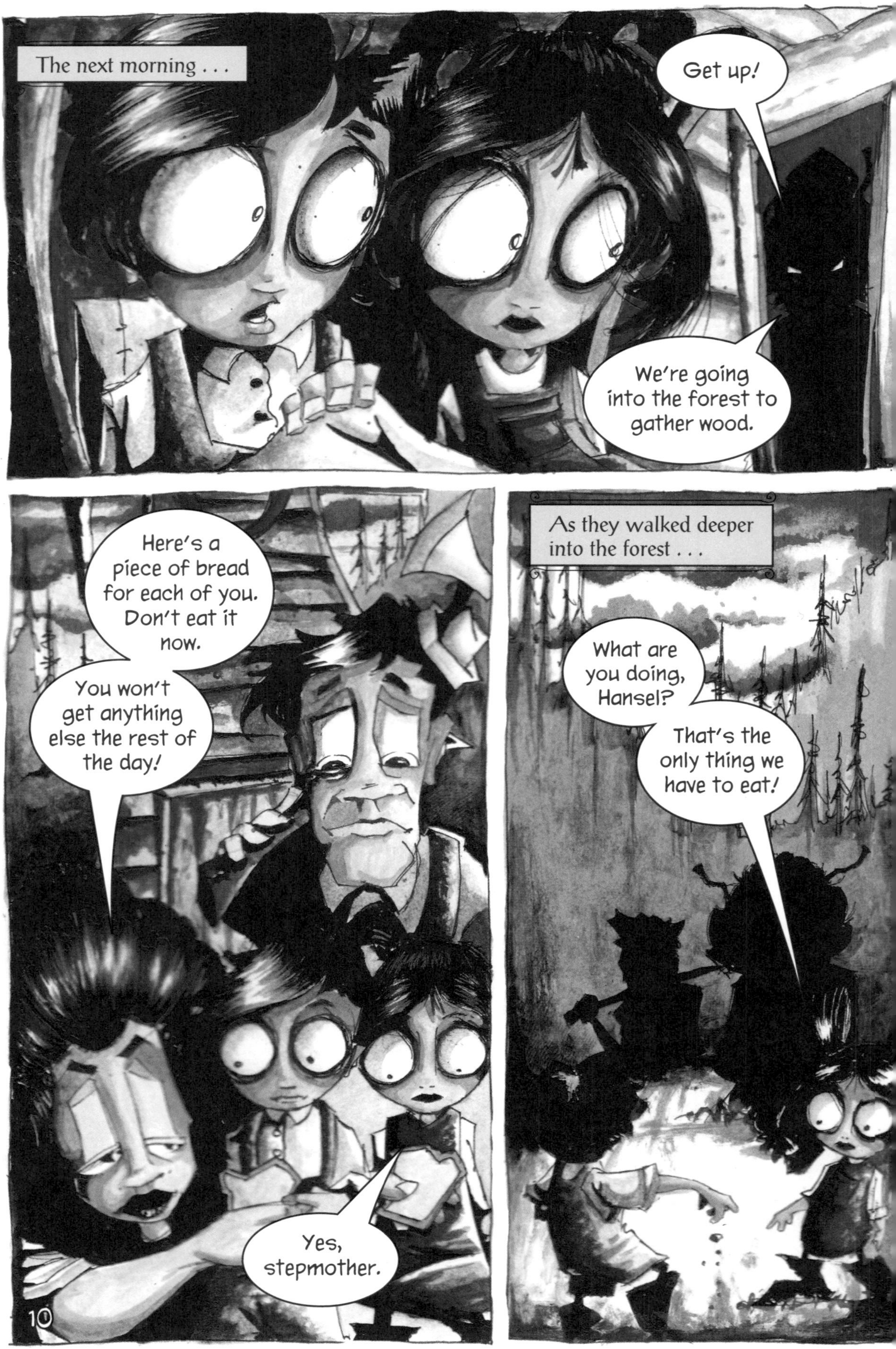

The next morning . . .
Get up!
We're going into the forest to gather wood.
Here's a piece of bread for each of you. Don't eat it now.
You won't get anything else the rest of the day!
Yes, stepmother.
As they walked deeper into the forest . . .
What are you doing, Hansel?
That's the only thing we have to eat!

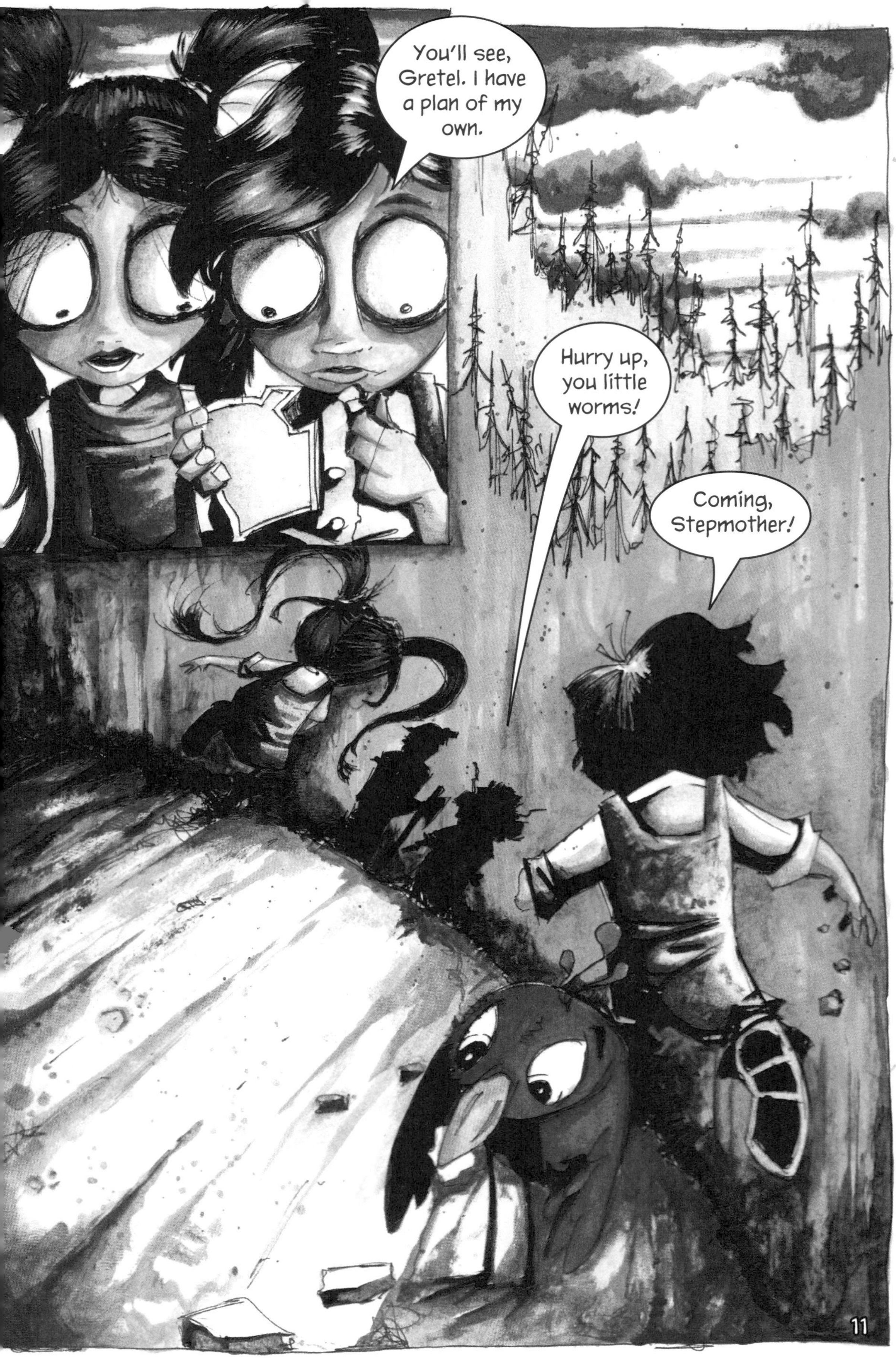
You'll see, Gretel. I have a plan of my own.
Hurry up, you little worms!
Coming, Stepmother!

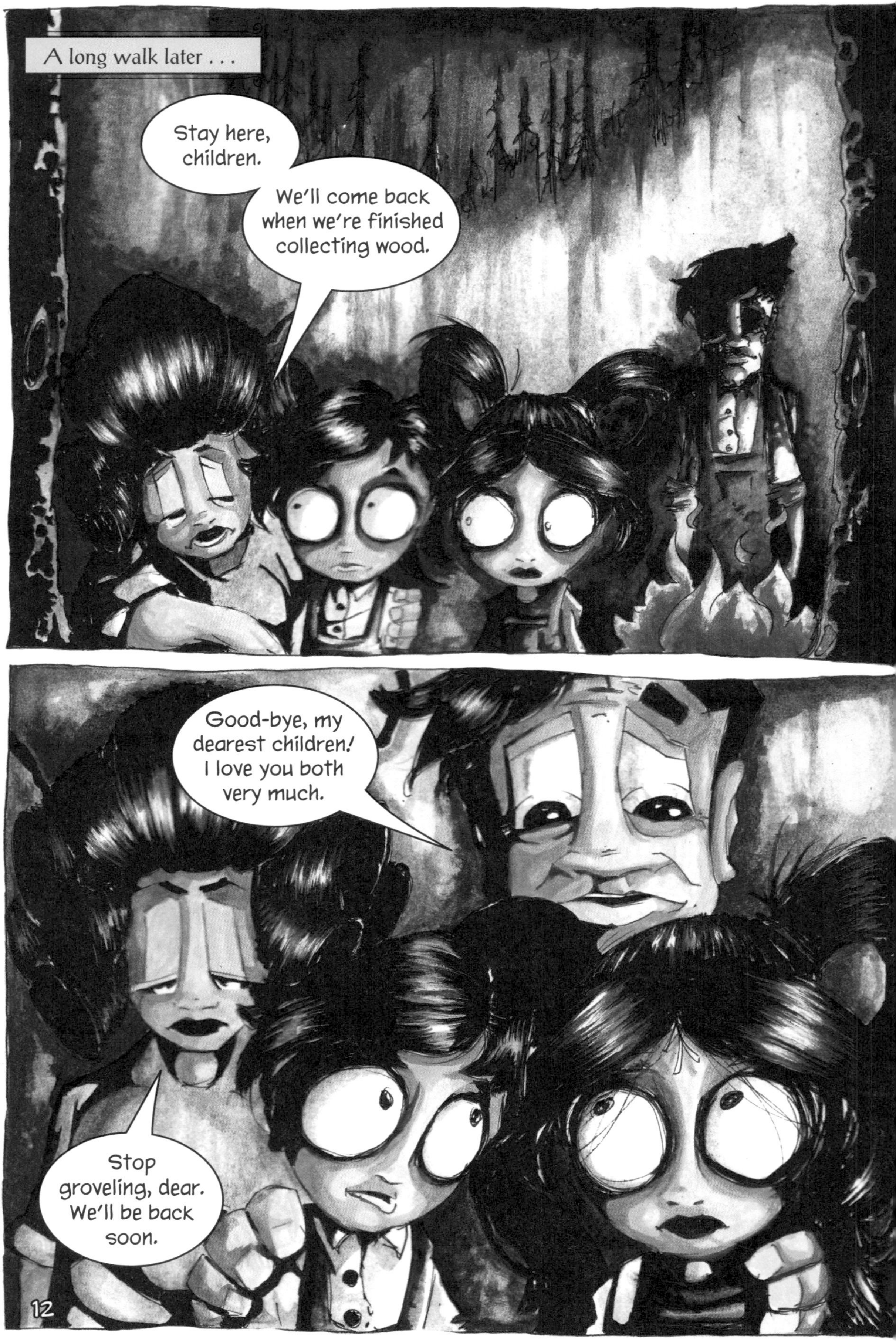
A long walk later . . .
Stay here, children.
We'll come back when we're finished collecting wood.
Good-bye, my dearest children! I love you both very much.
Stop groveling, dear. We'll be back soon.

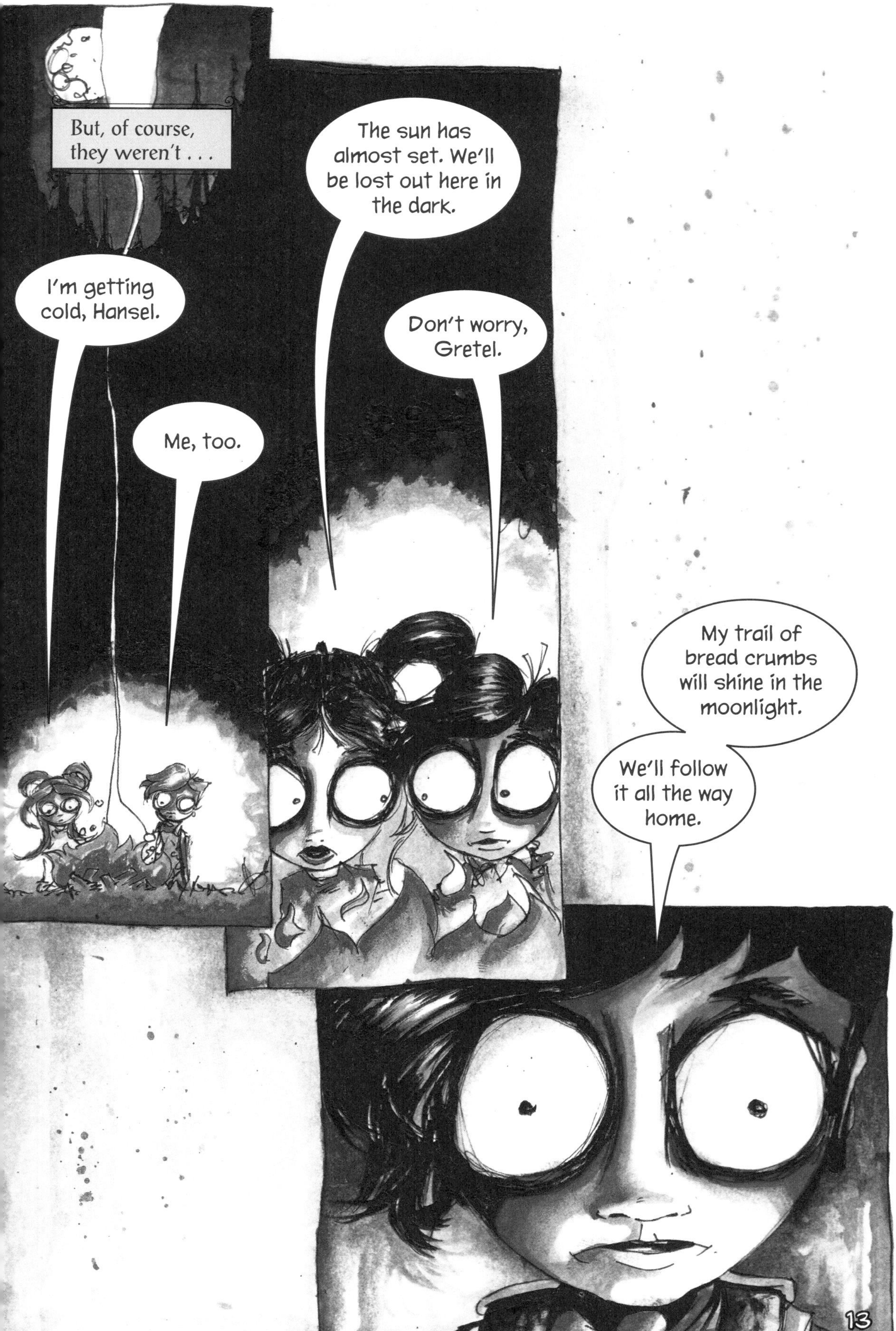
But, of course, they weren't . . .
I'm getting cold, Hansel.
Me, too.
The sun has almost set. We'll be lost out here in the dark.
Don't worry, Gretel.
My trail of bread crumbs will shine in the moonlight.
We'll follow it all the way home.

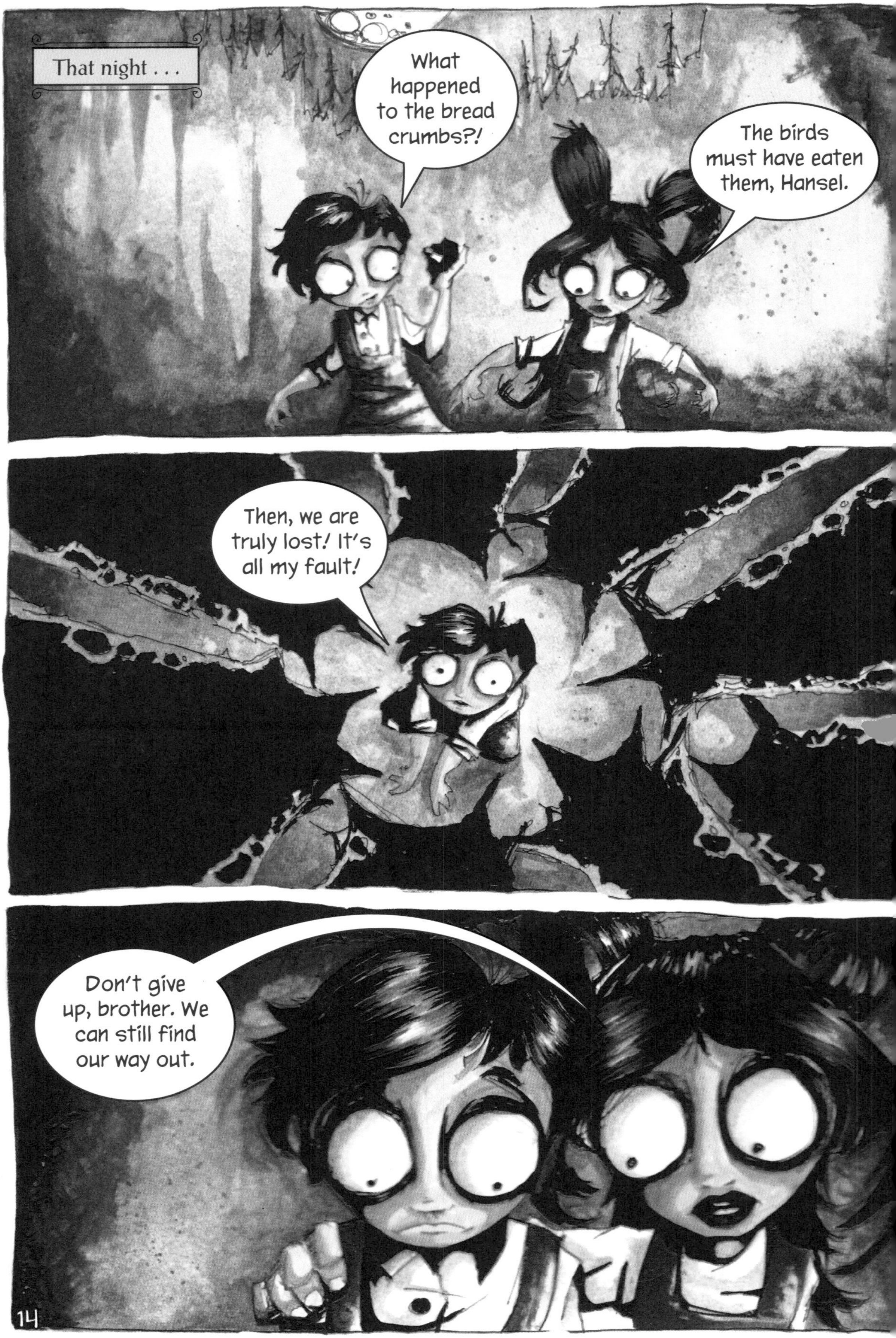
That night . . .
What happened to the bread crumbs?!
The birds must have eaten them, Hansel.
Then, we are truly lost! It's all my fault!
Don't give up, brother. We can still find our way out.

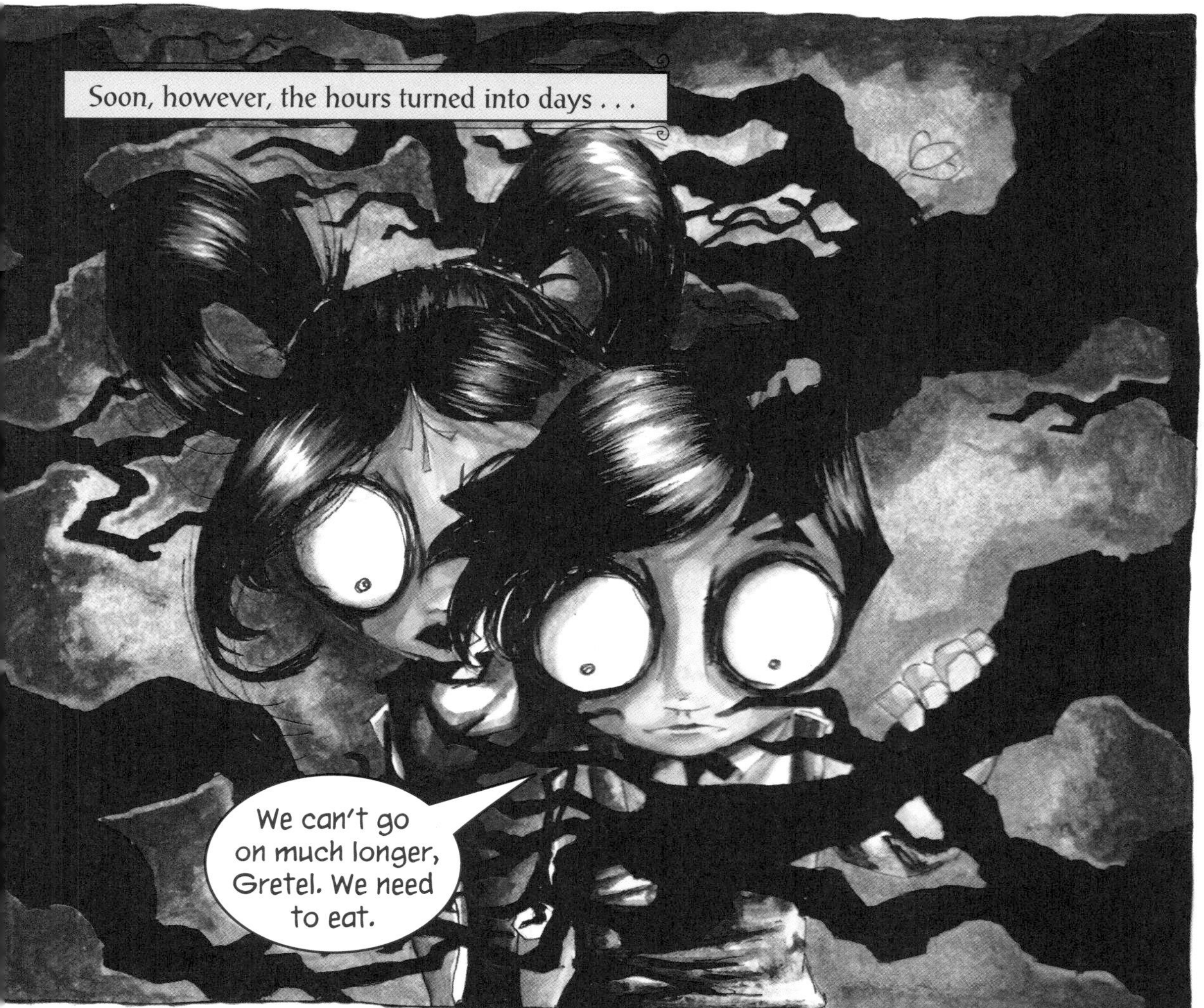
Soon, however, the hours turned into days . . .
We can't go on much longer, Gretel. We need to eat.

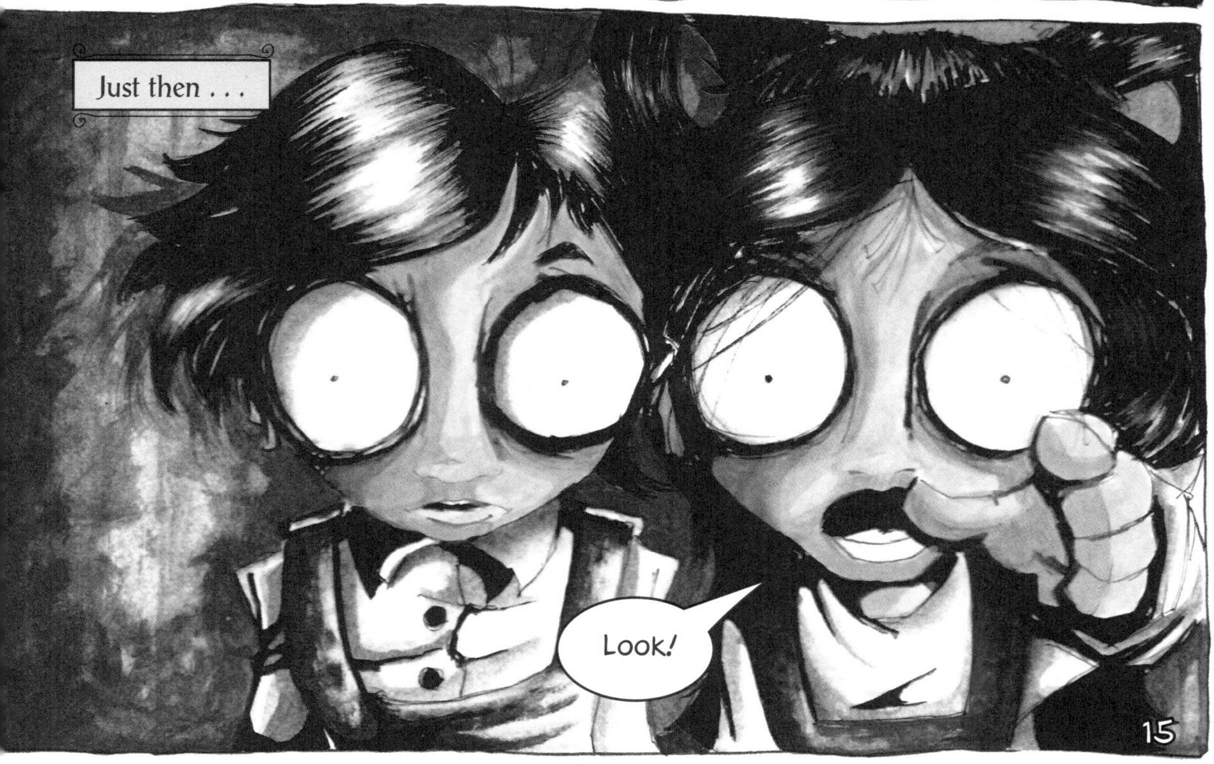
Just then . . .
Look!

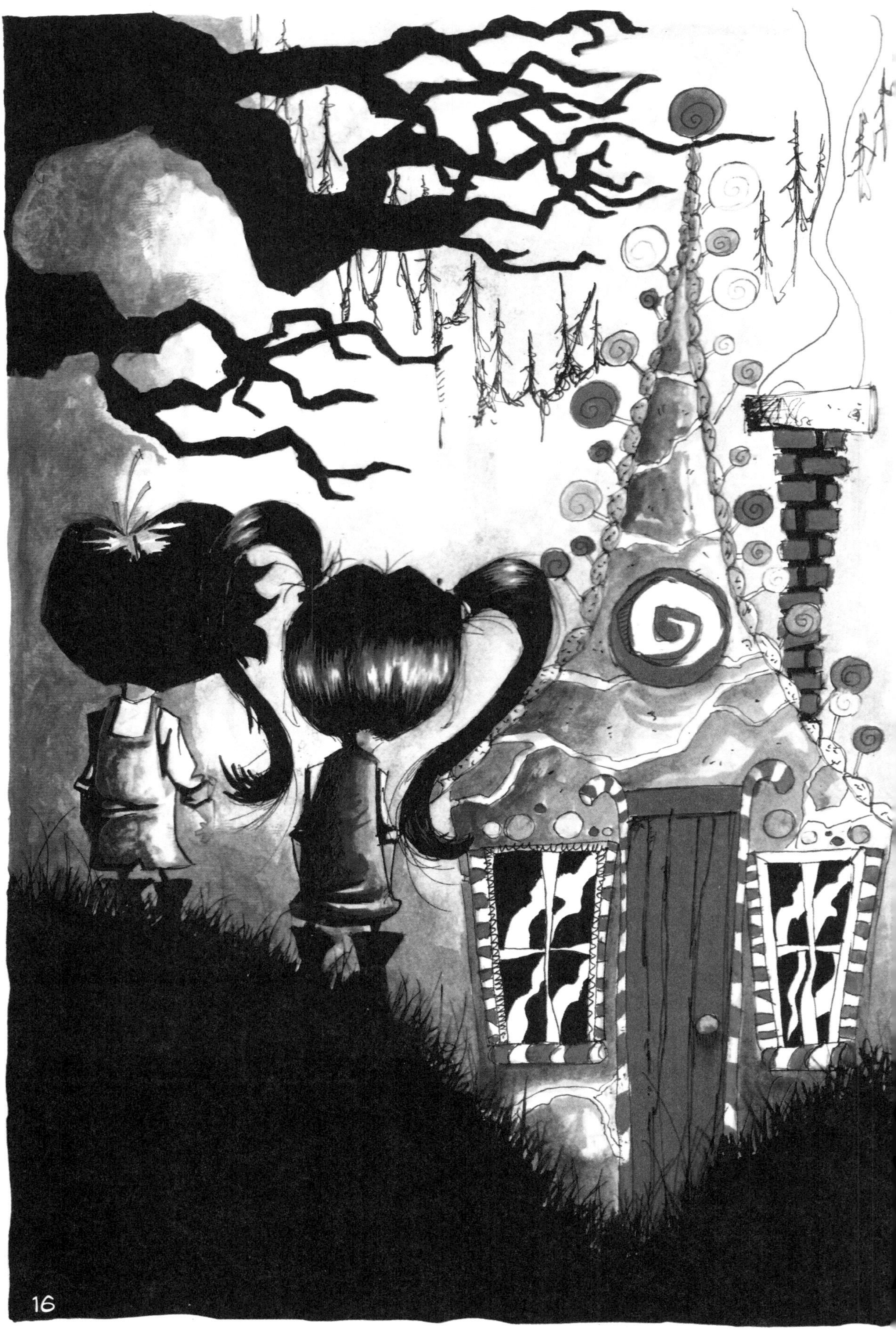

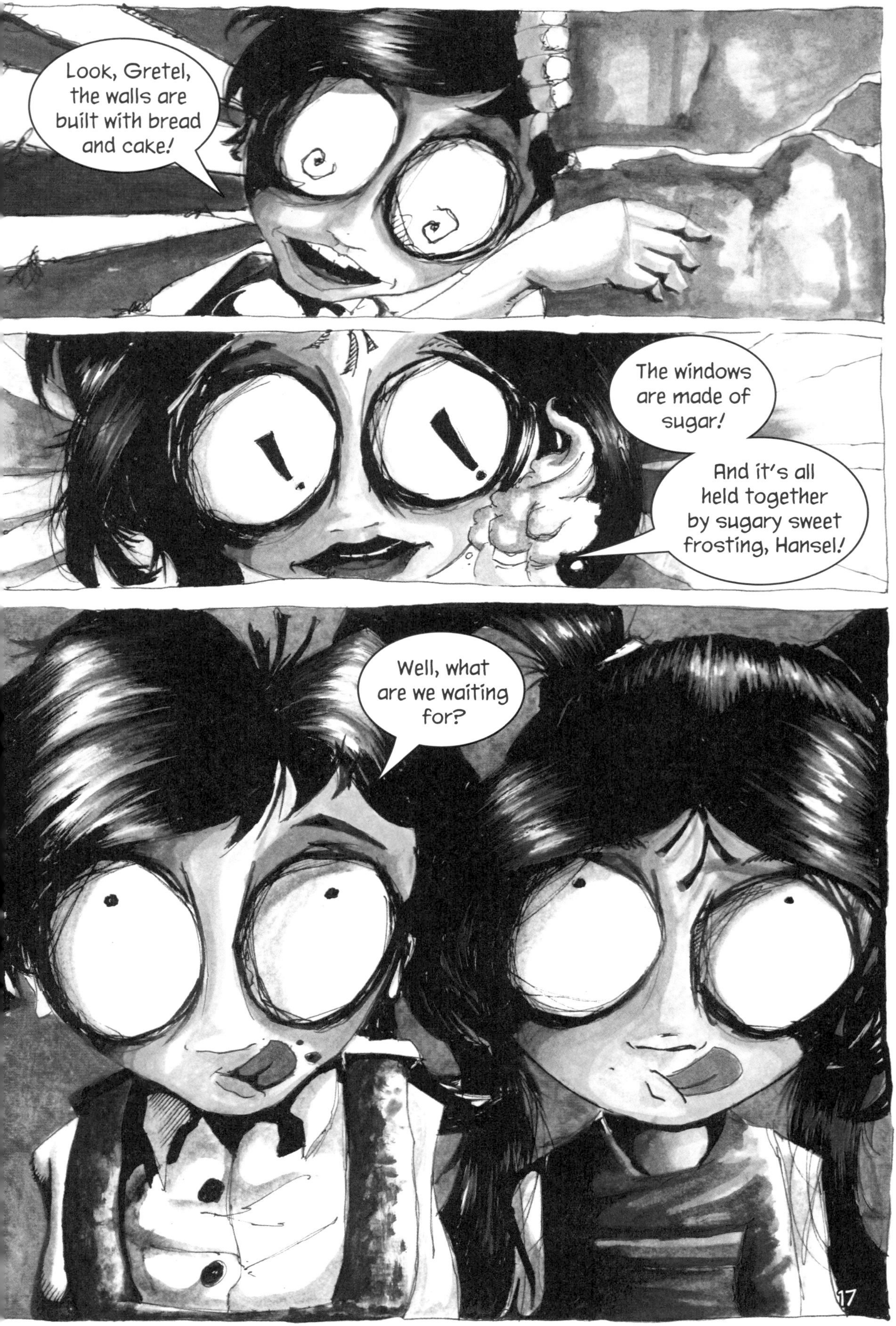
Look, Gretel, the walls are built with bread and cake!
The windows are made of sugar!
And it's all held together by sugary sweet frosting, Hansel!
Well, what are we waiting for?

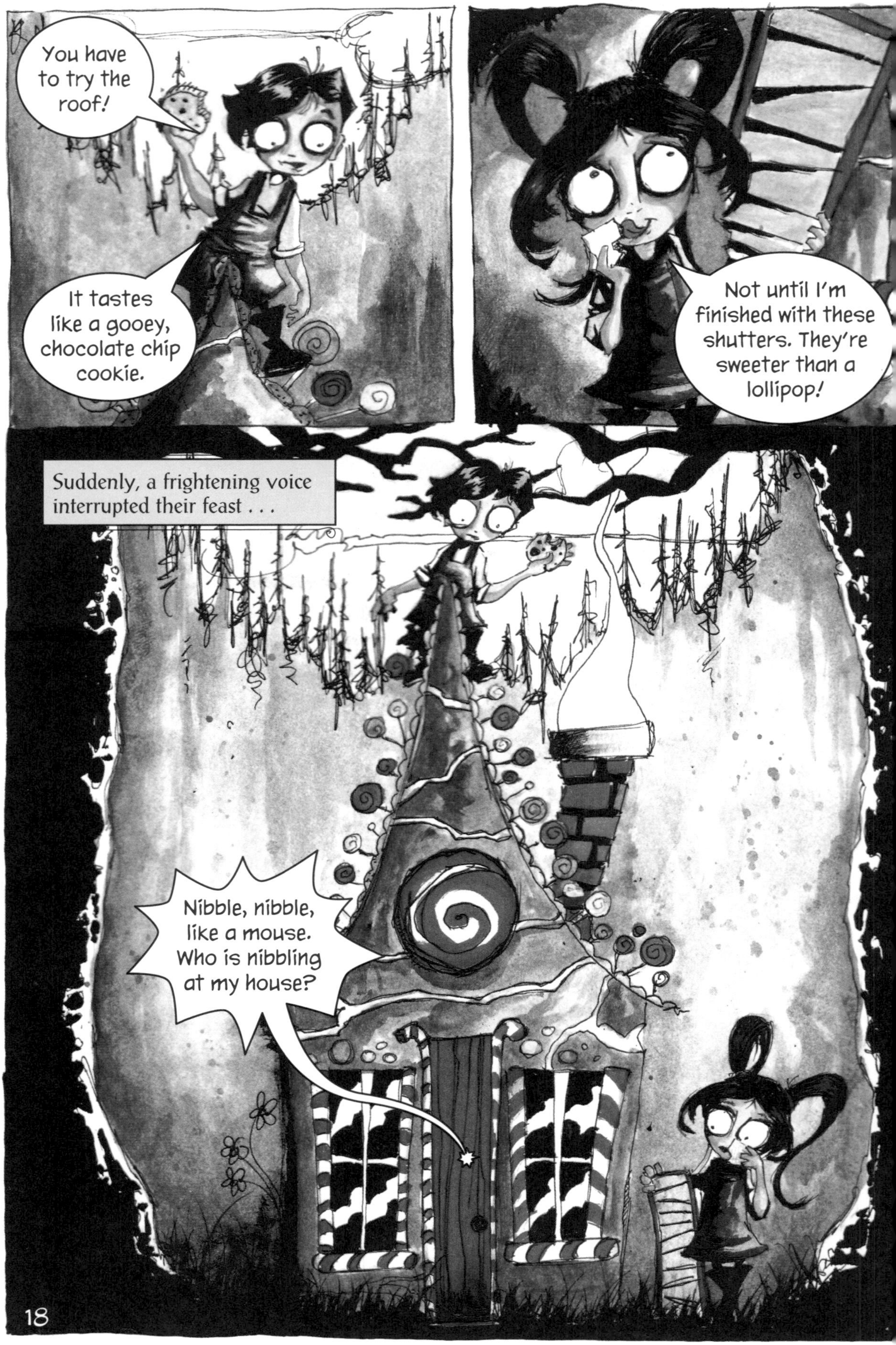
You have to try the roof!
It tastes like a gooey, chocolate chip cookie.
Not until I'm finished with these shutters. They're sweeter than a lollipop!
Suddenly, a frightening voice interrupted their feast . . .
Nibble, nibble, like a mouse. Who is nibbling at my house?

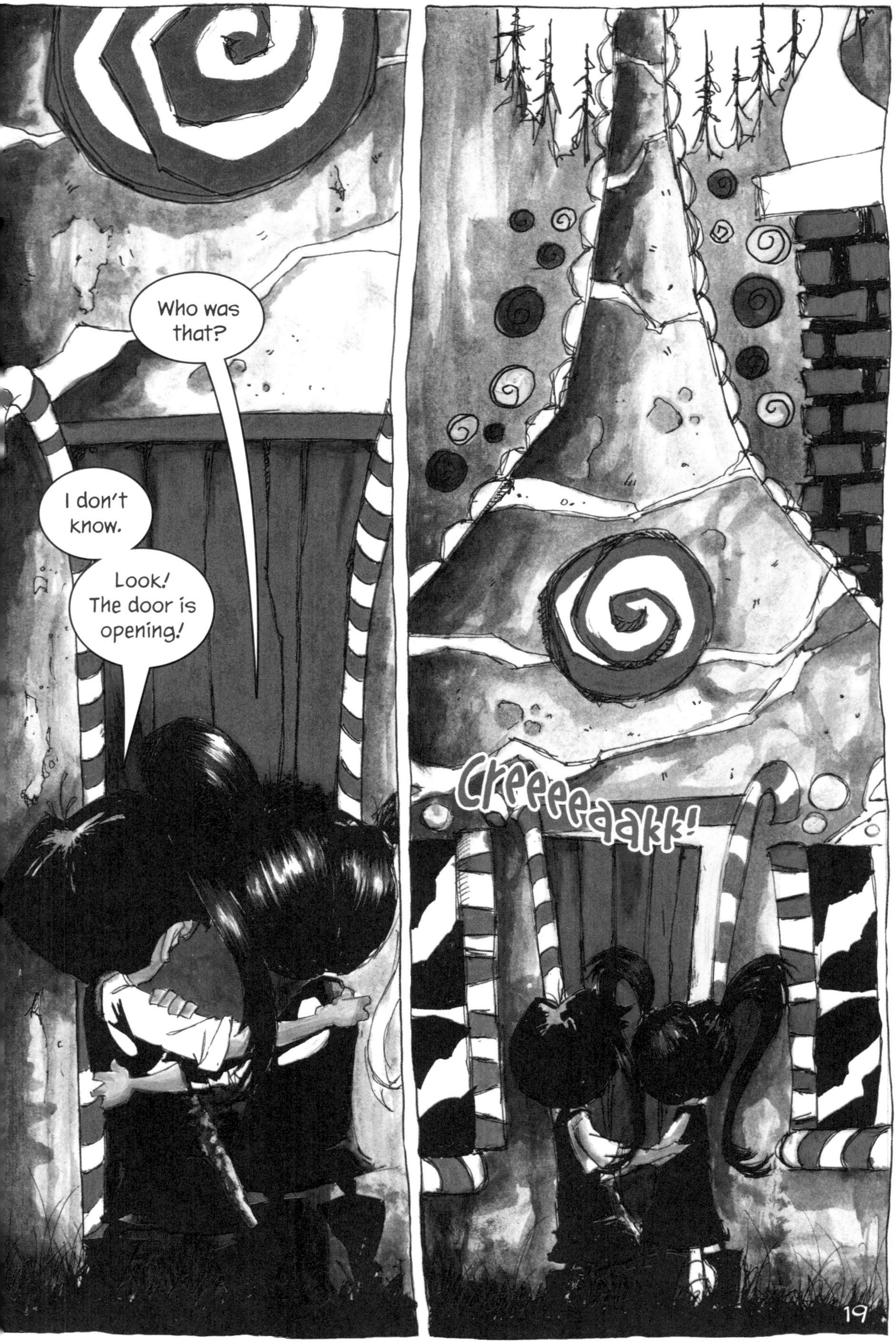
Who was that?
I don't know.
Look! The door is opening!
Creeeeaakk!

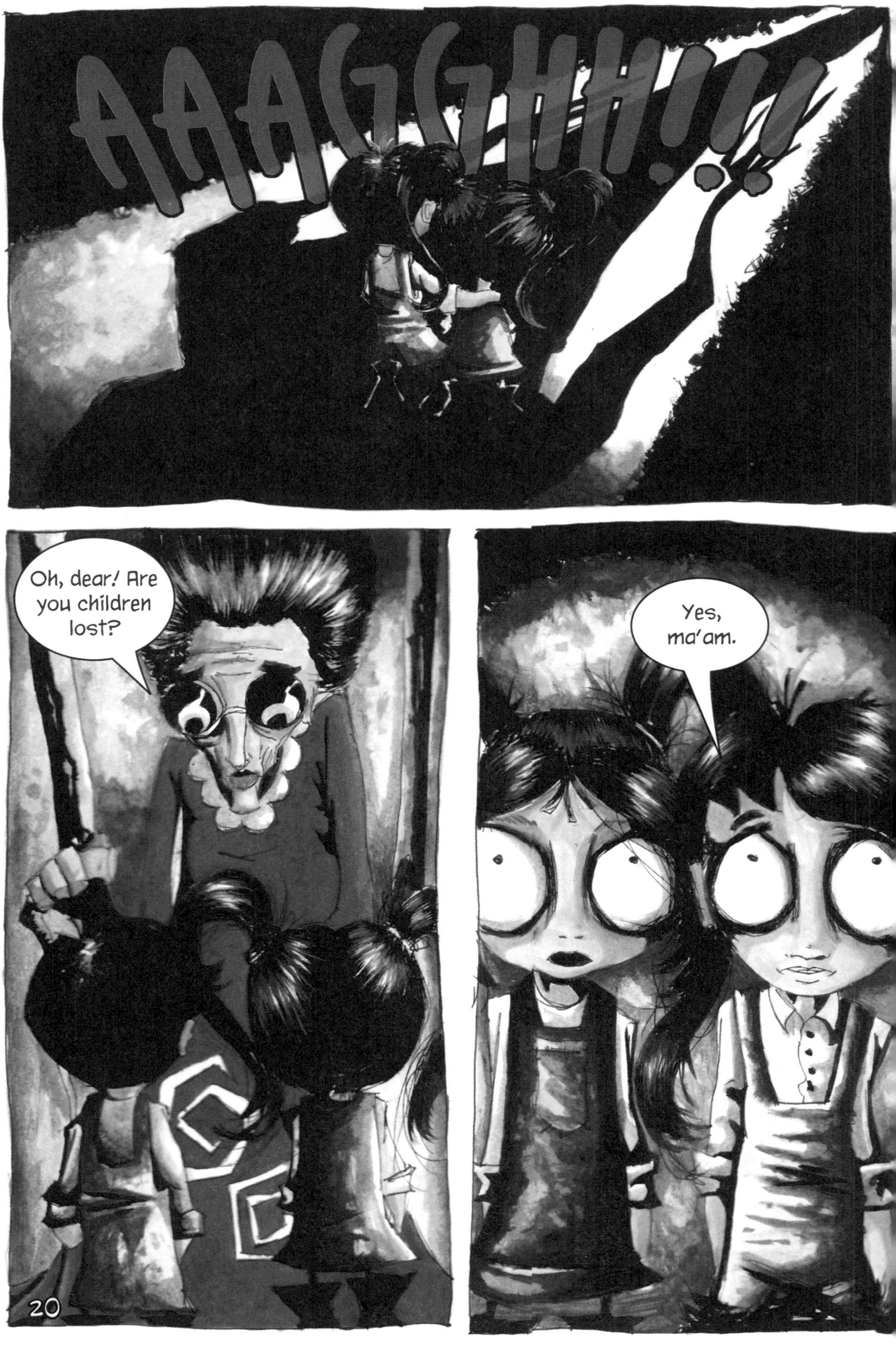
AAAGGHH!!!
Oh, dear! Are you children lost?
Yes, ma'am.

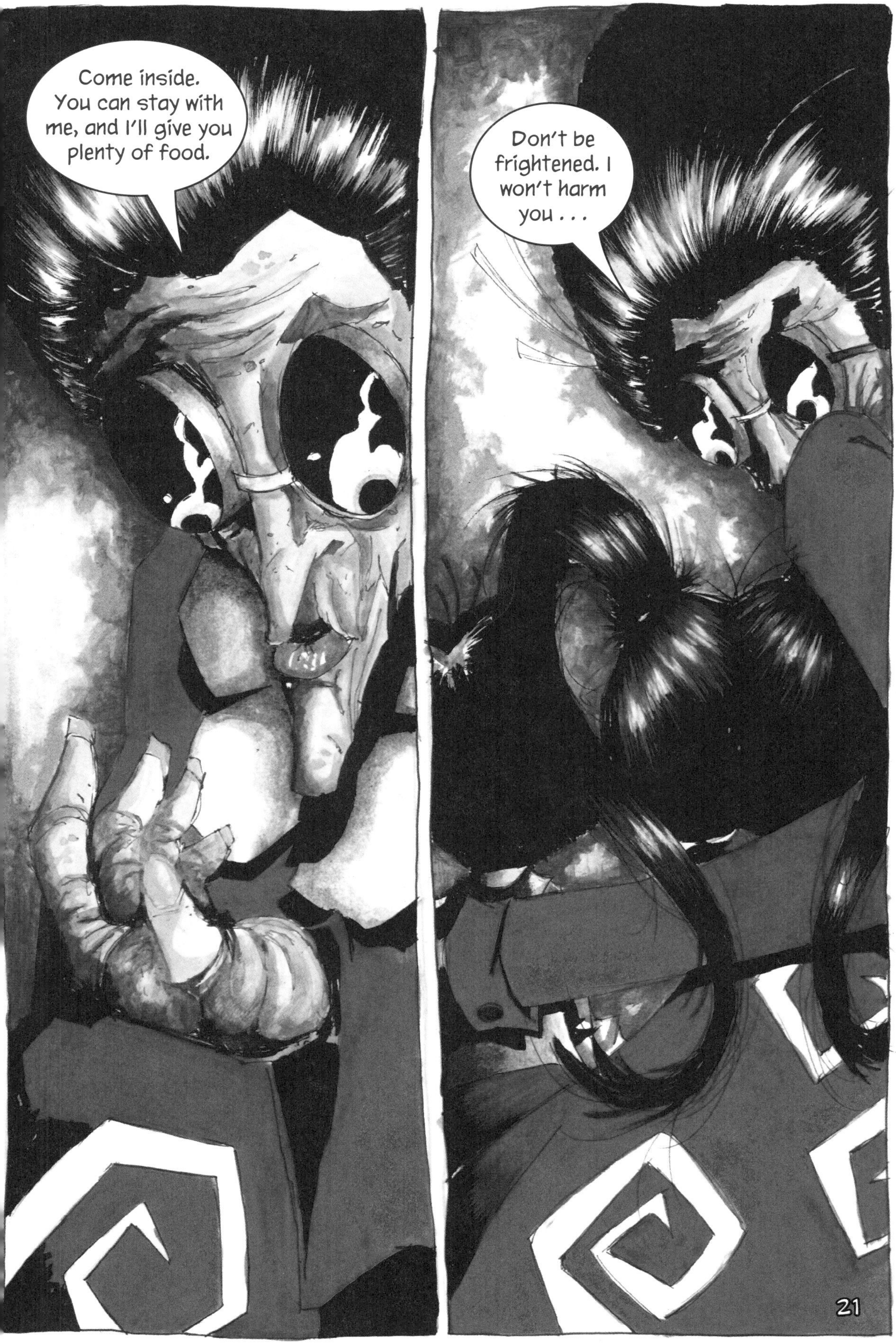
Come inside. You can stay with me, and I'll give you plenty of food.
Don't be frightened. I won't harm you . . .

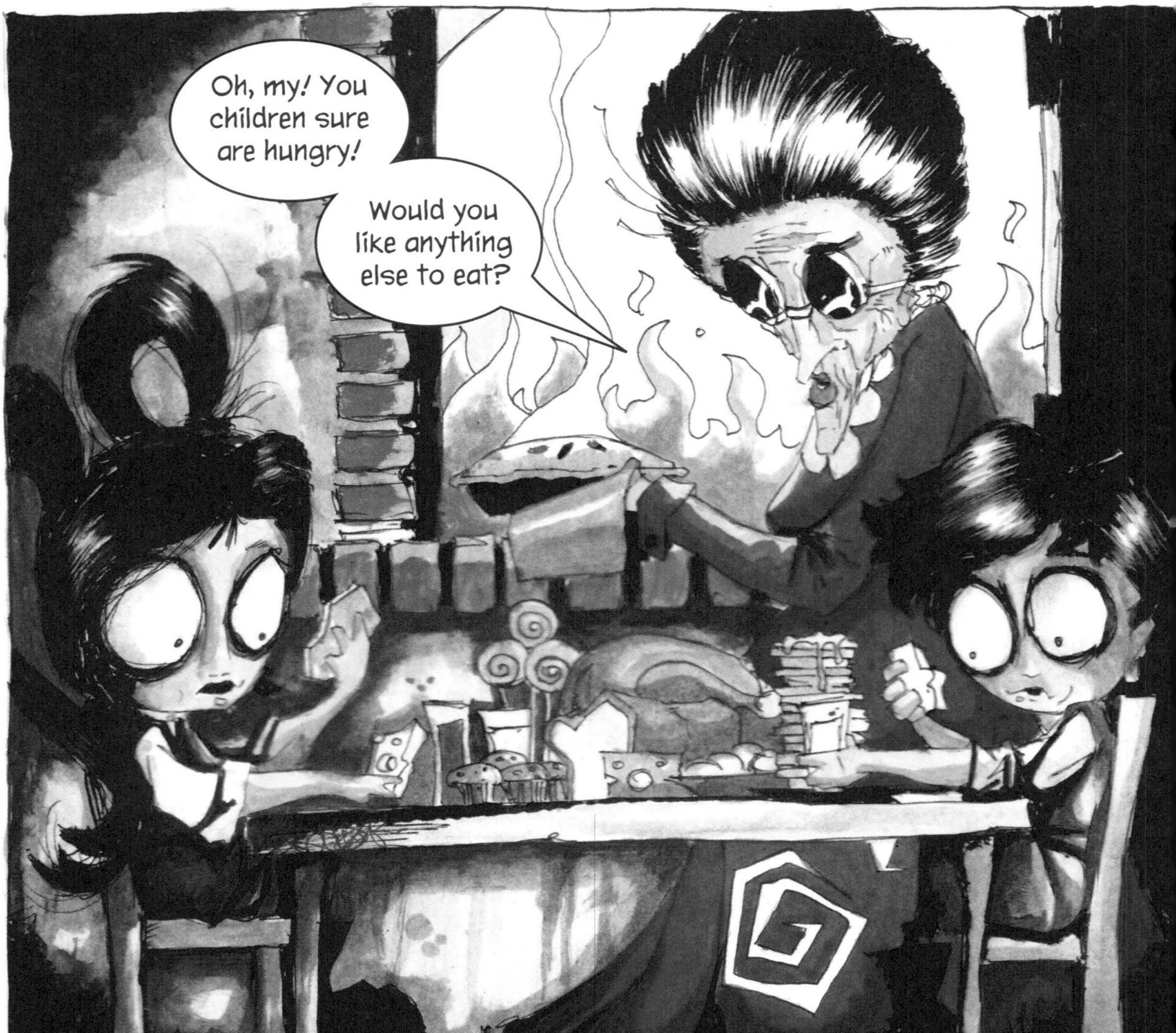
Oh, my! You children sure are hungry!
Would you like anything else to eat?

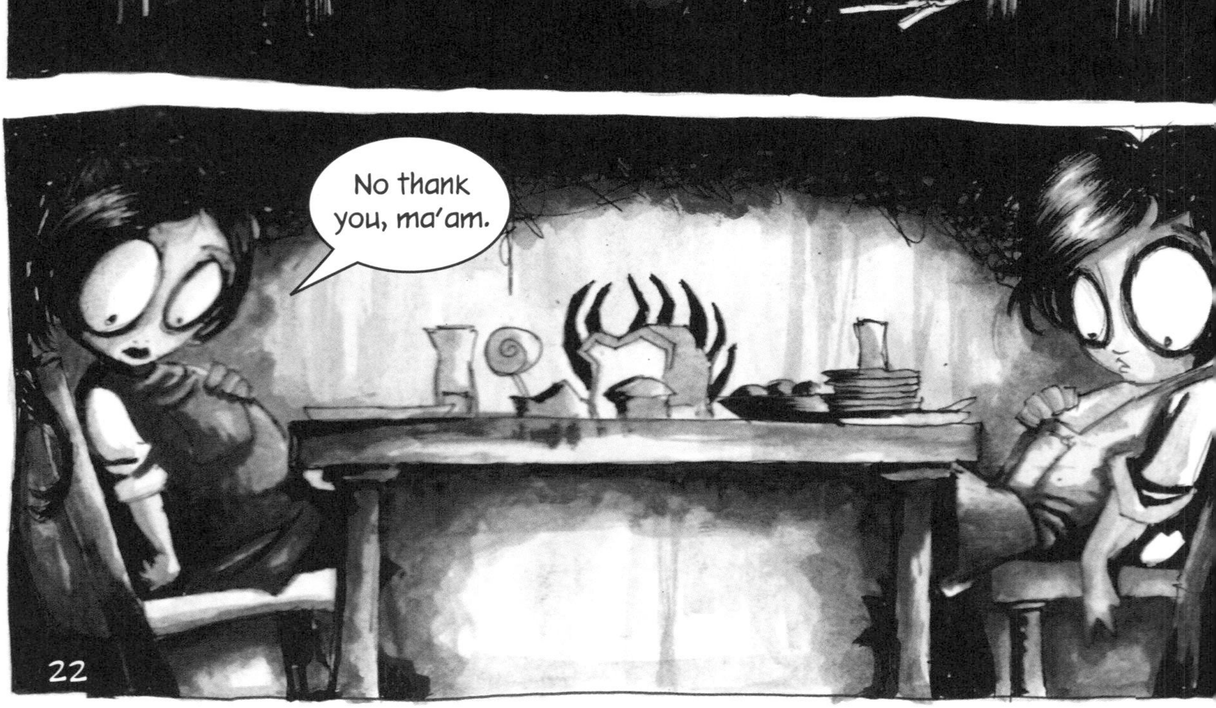
No thank you, ma'am.

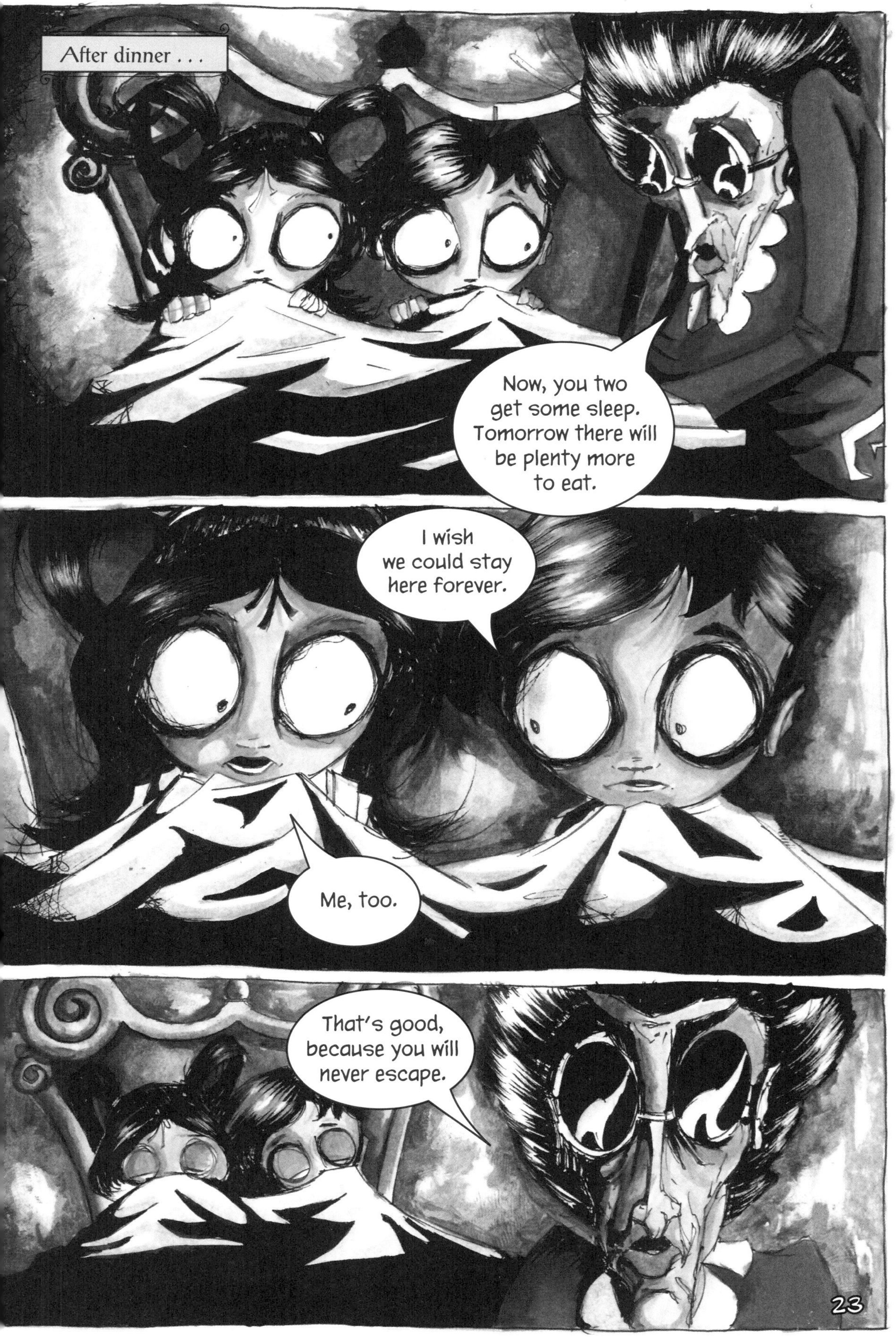
After dinner . . .
Now, you two get some sleep. Tomorrow there will be plenty more to eat.
I wish we could stay here forever.
Me, too.
That's good, because you will never escape.

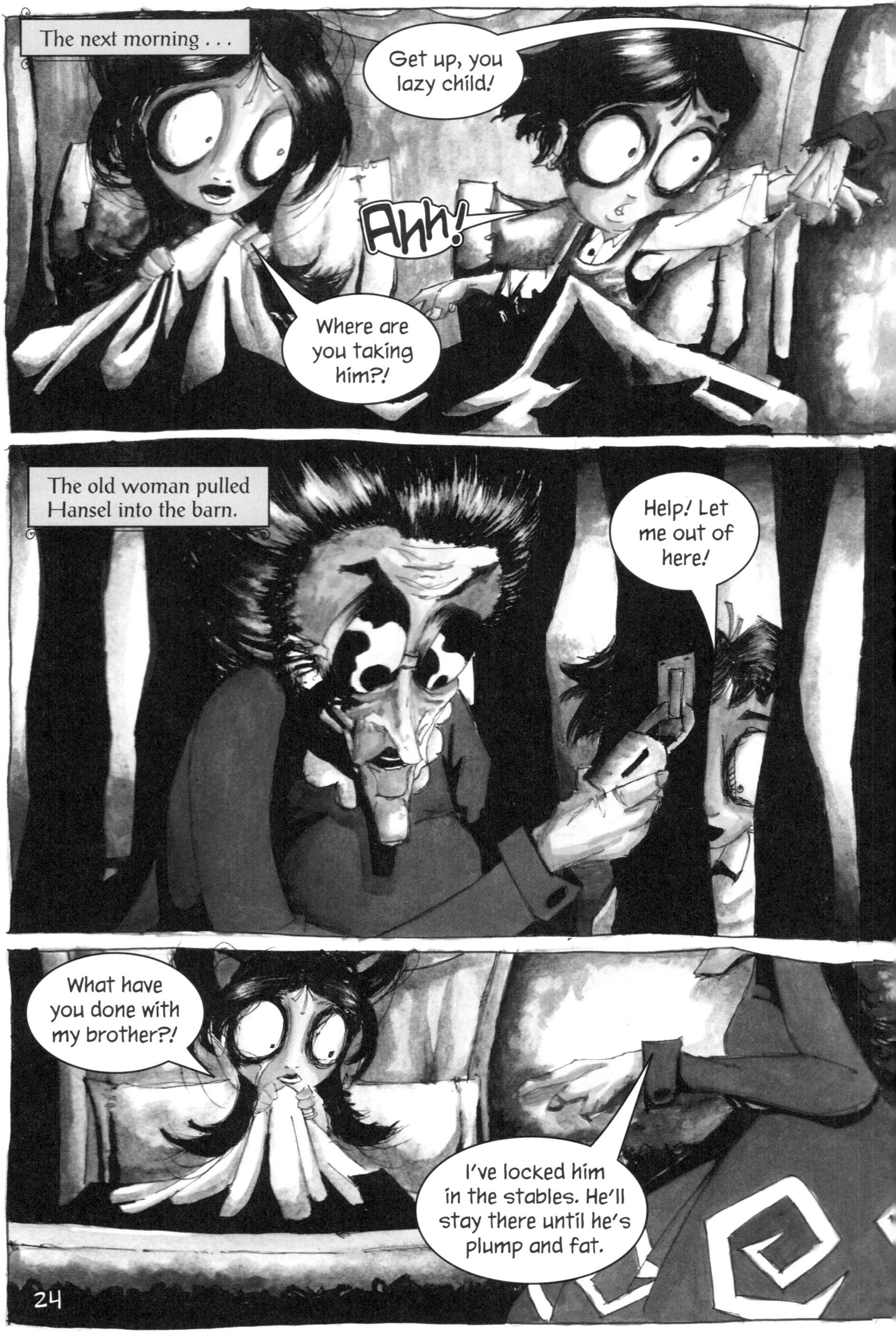
The next morning . . .
Get up, you lazy child!
Ahh!
Where are you taking him?!
The old woman pulled Hansel into the barn.
Help! Let me out of here!
What have you done with my brother?!
I've locked him in the stables. He'll stay there until he's plump and fat.

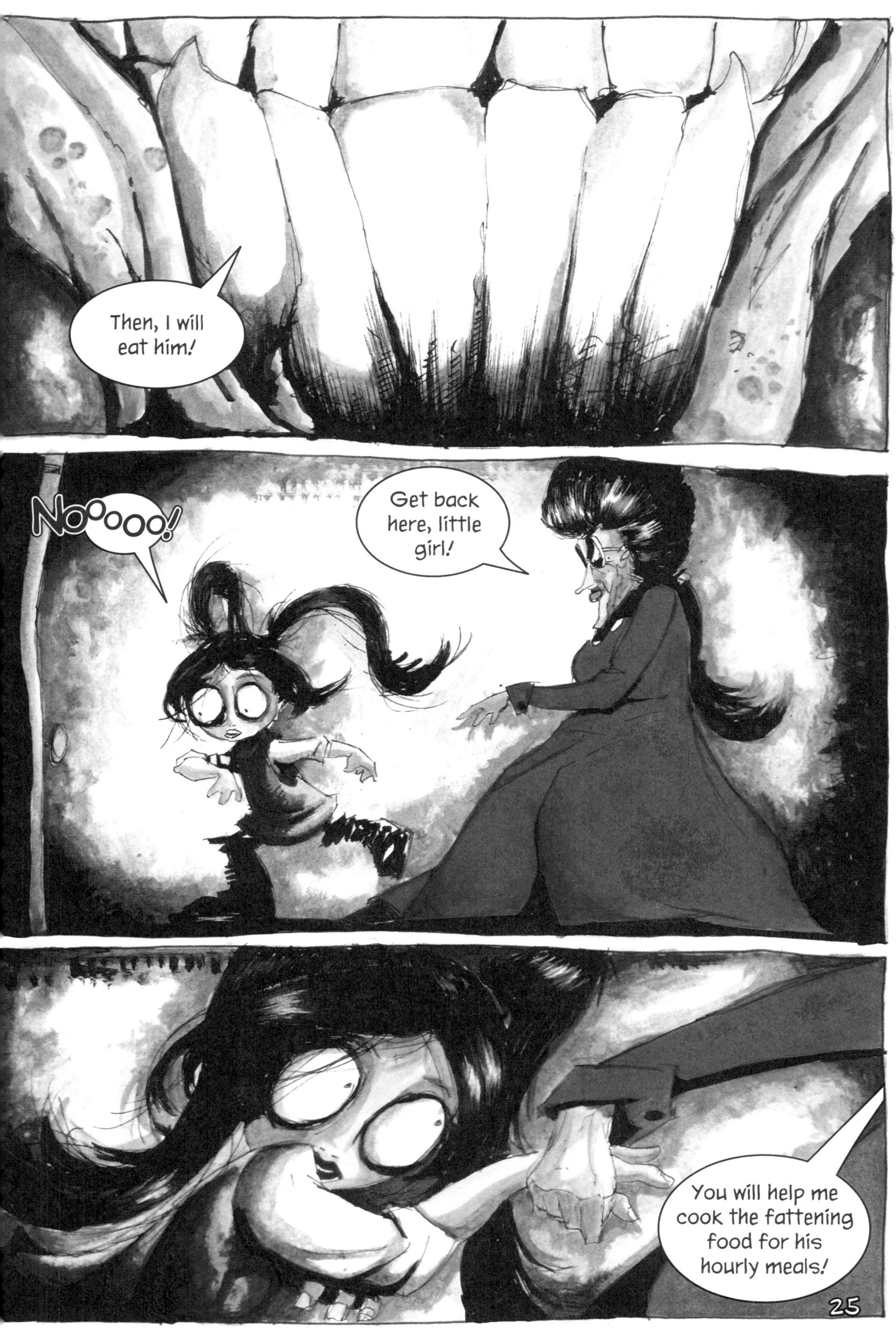
Then, I will eat him!
Noooooo!
Get back here, little girl!
You will help me cook the fattening food for his hourly meals!

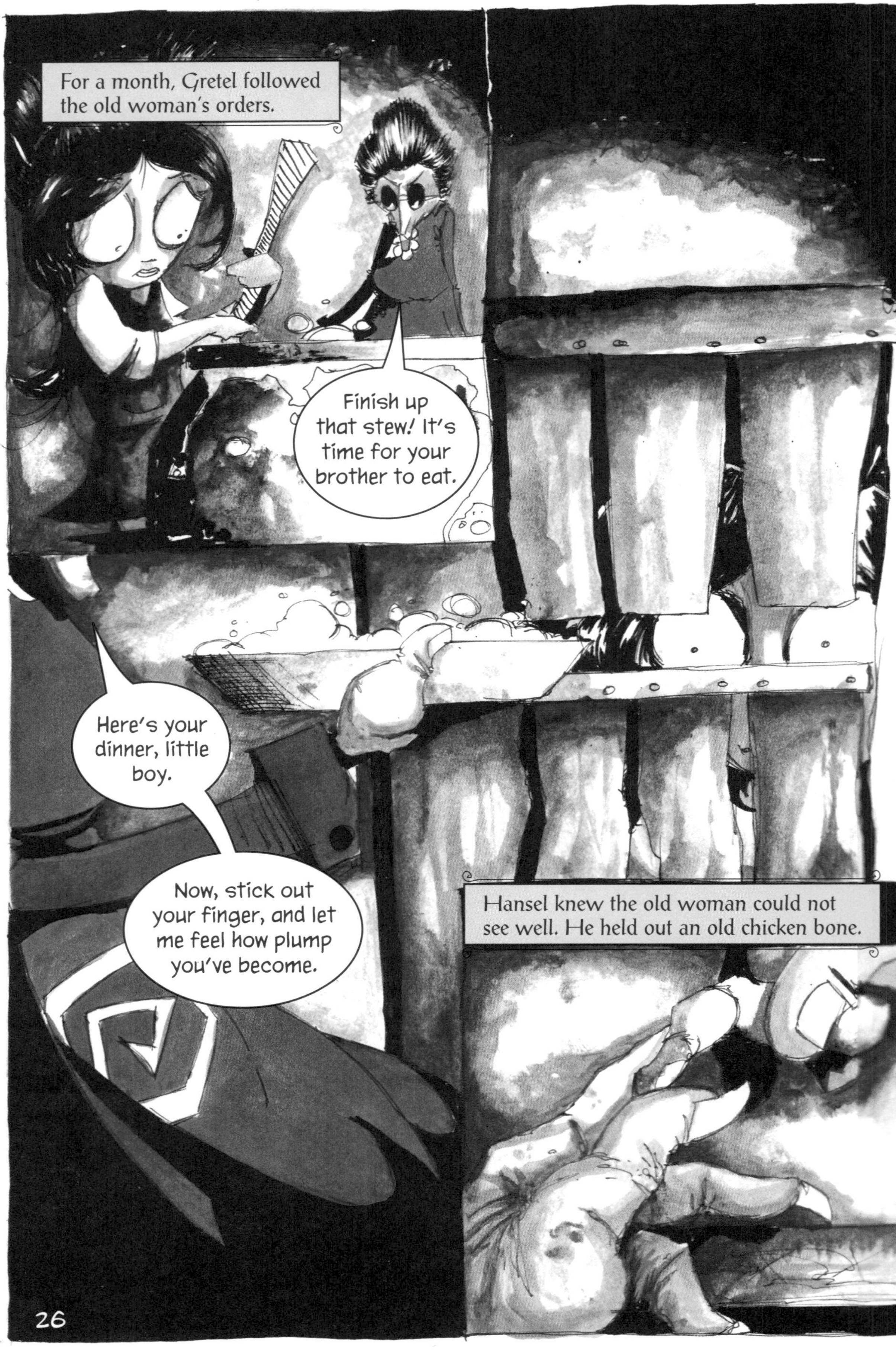

For a month, Gretel followed the old woman's orders.
Finish up that stew! It's time for your brother to eat.
Here's your dinner, little boy.
Now, stick out your finger, and let me feel how plump you've become.
Hansel knew the old woman could not see well. He held out an old chicken bone.

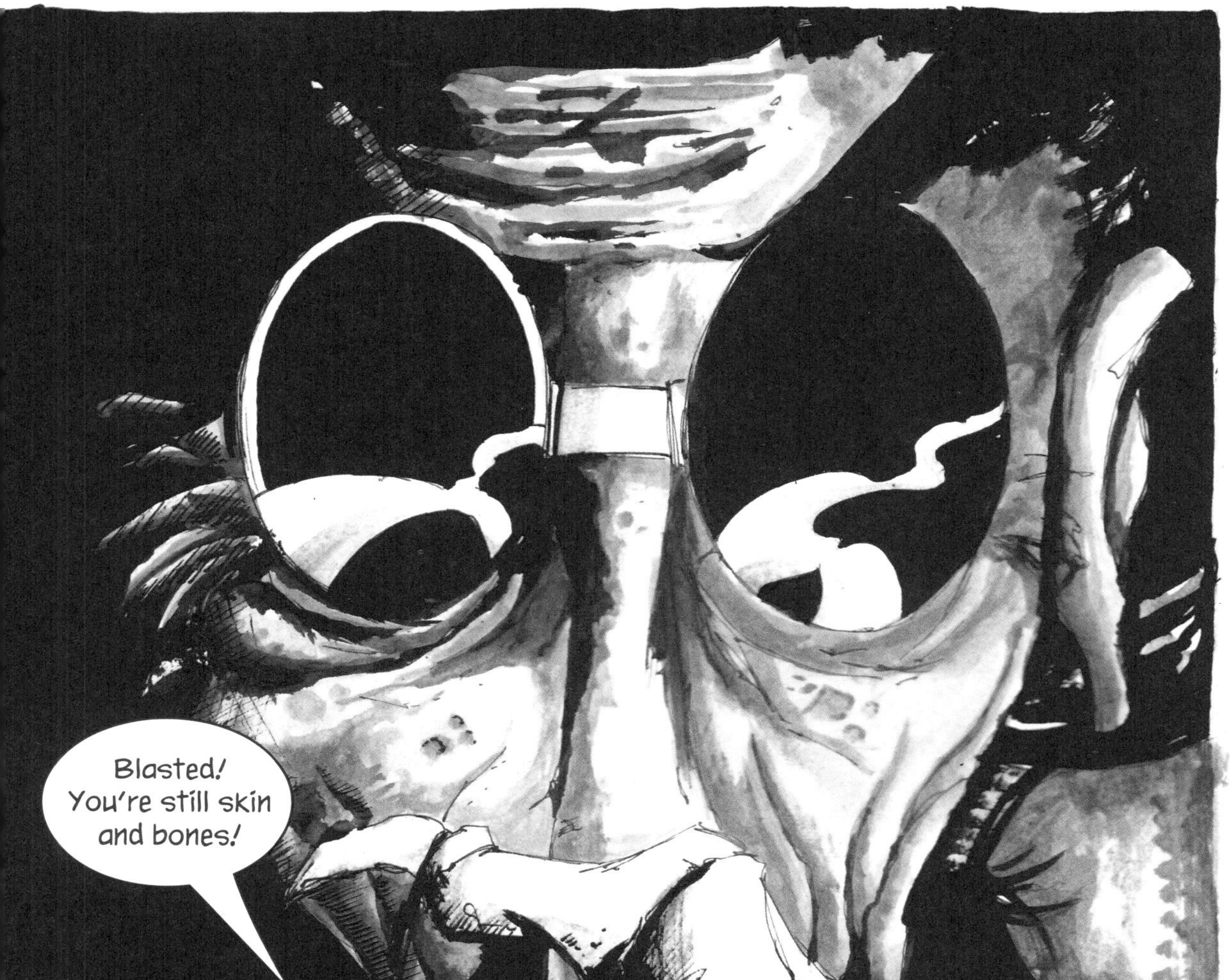
Blasted! You're still skin and bones!

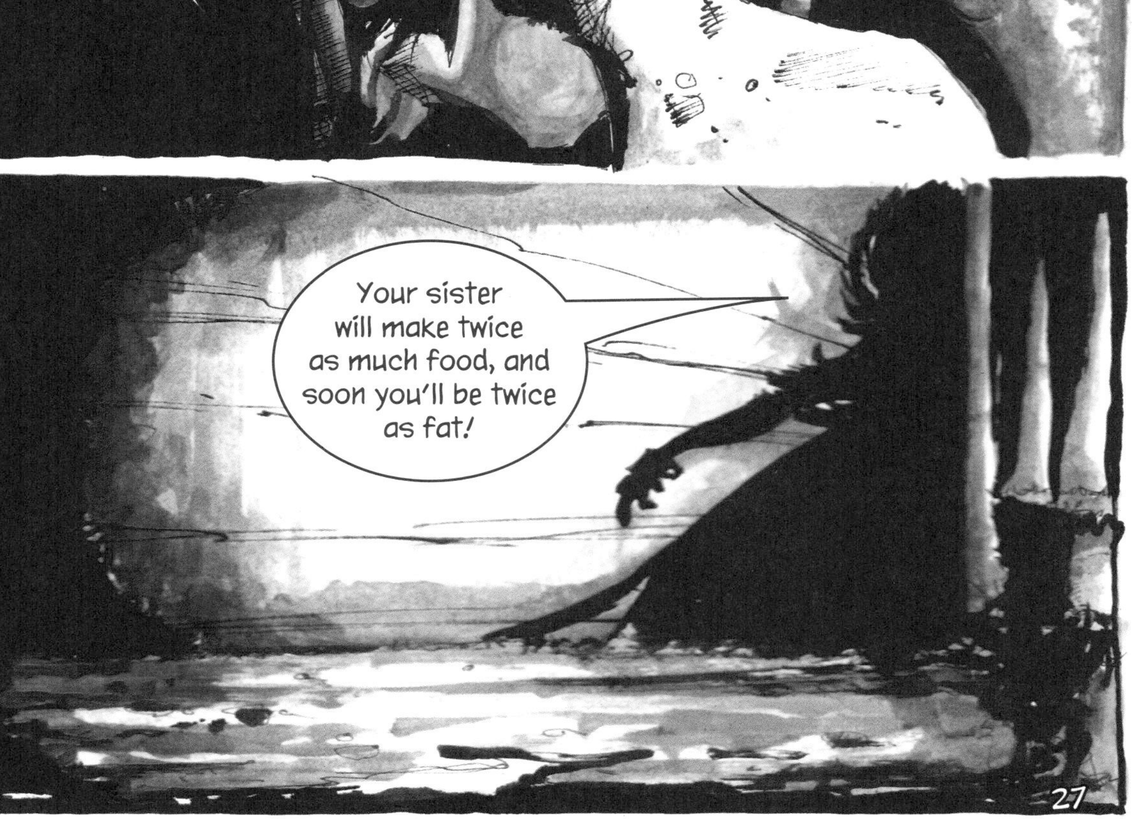
Your sister will make twice as much food, and soon you'll be twice as fat!

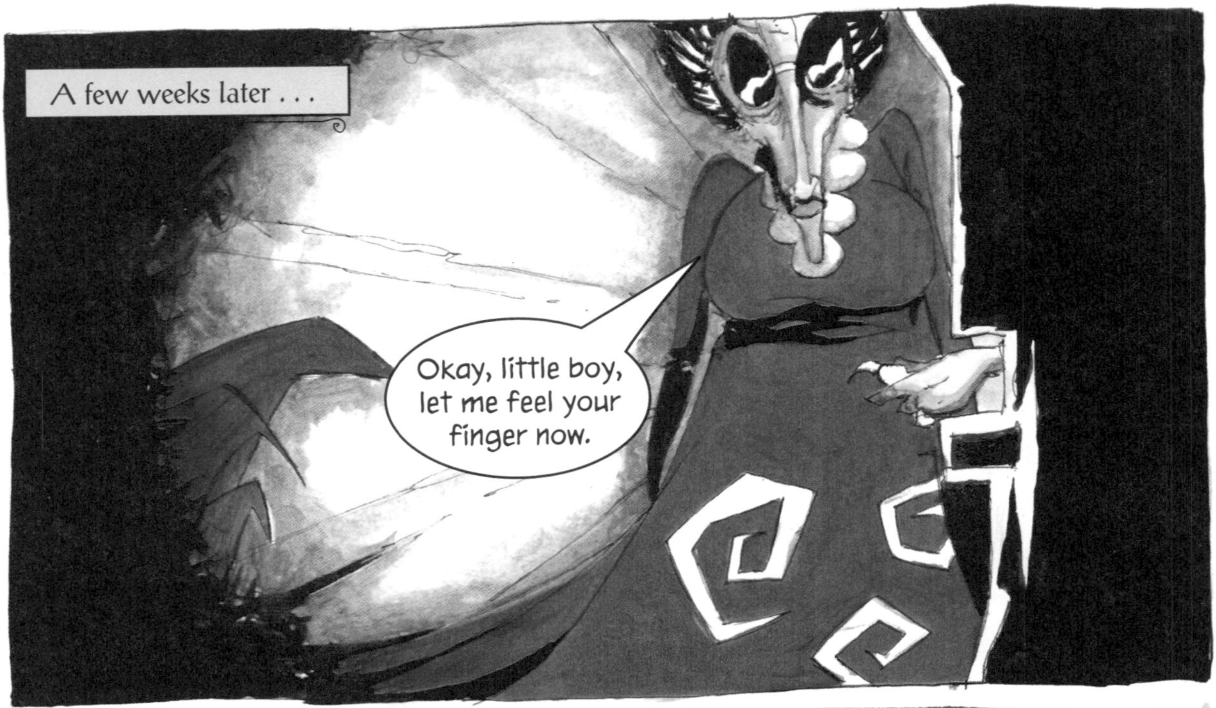
A few weeks later . . .
Okay, little boy, let me feel your finger now.

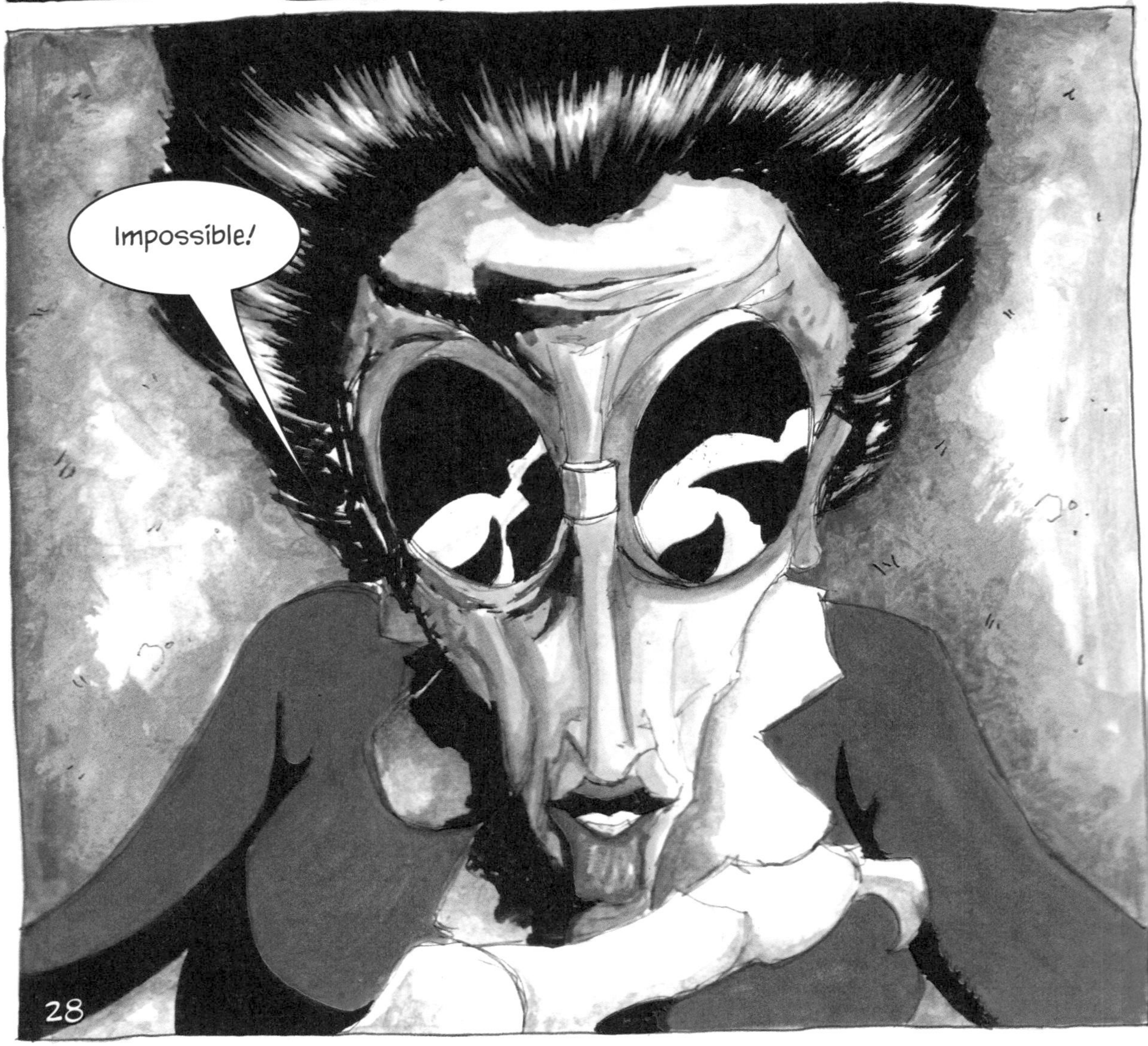
Impossible!

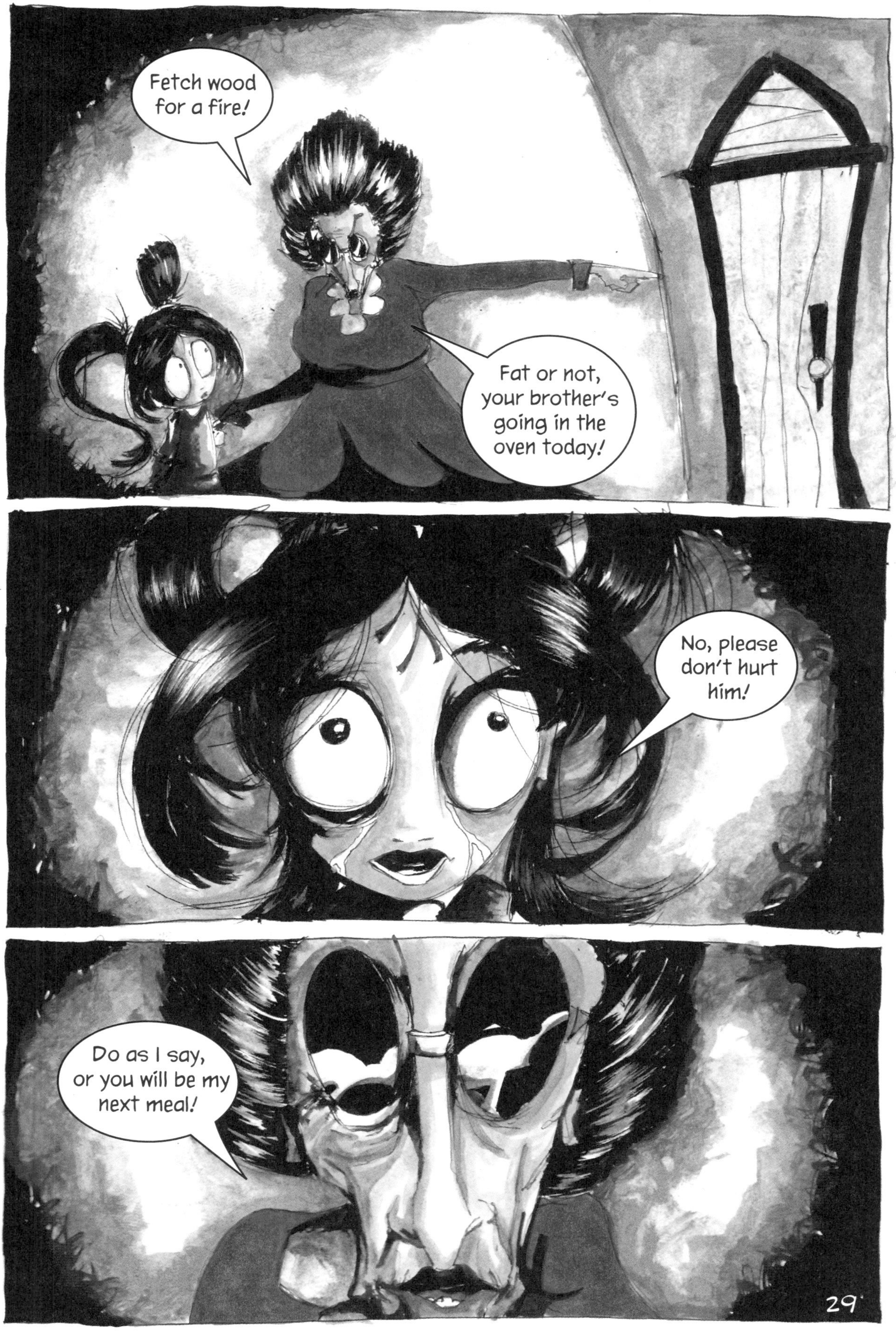
Fetch wood for a fire!
Fat or not, your brother's going in the oven today!
No, please don't hurt him!
Do as I say, or you will be my next meal!

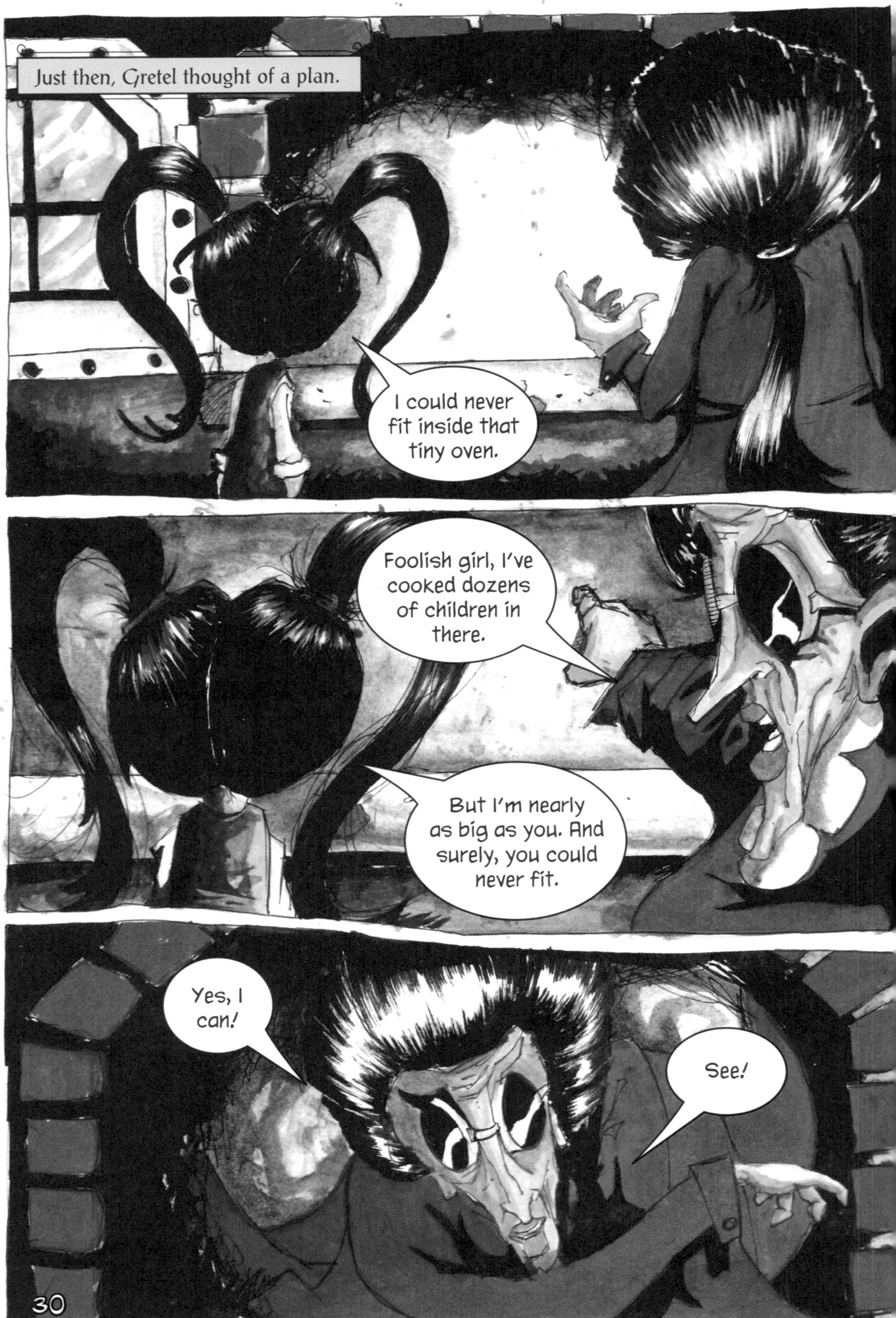
Just then, Gretel thought of a plan.
I could never fit inside that tiny oven.
Foolish girl, I've cooked dozens of children in there.
But I'm nearly as big as you. And surely, you could never fit.
Yes, I can!
See!

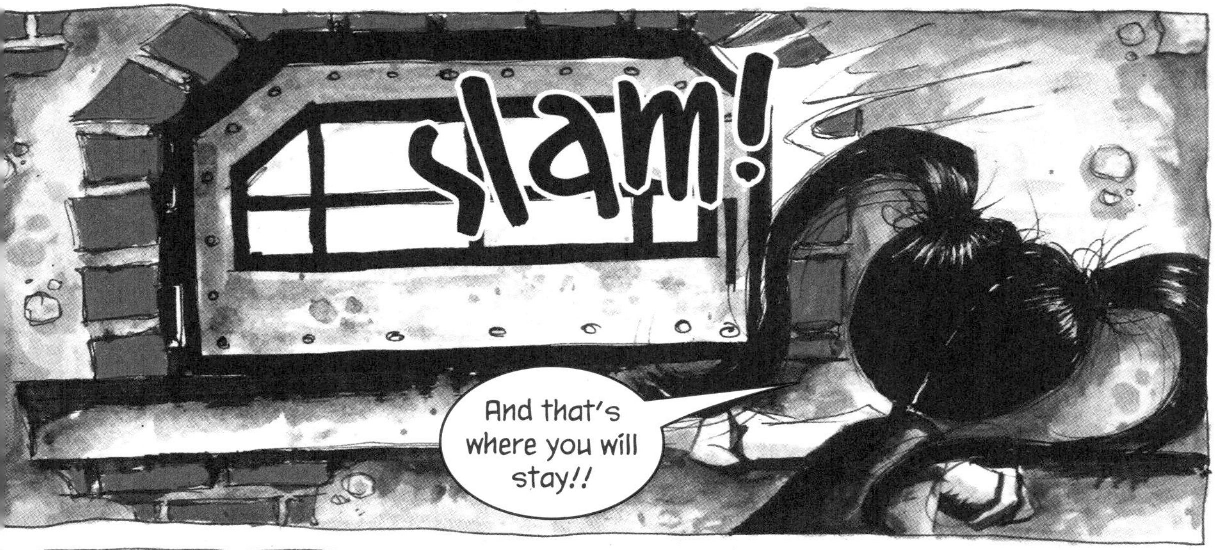
slam!
And that's where you will stay!!

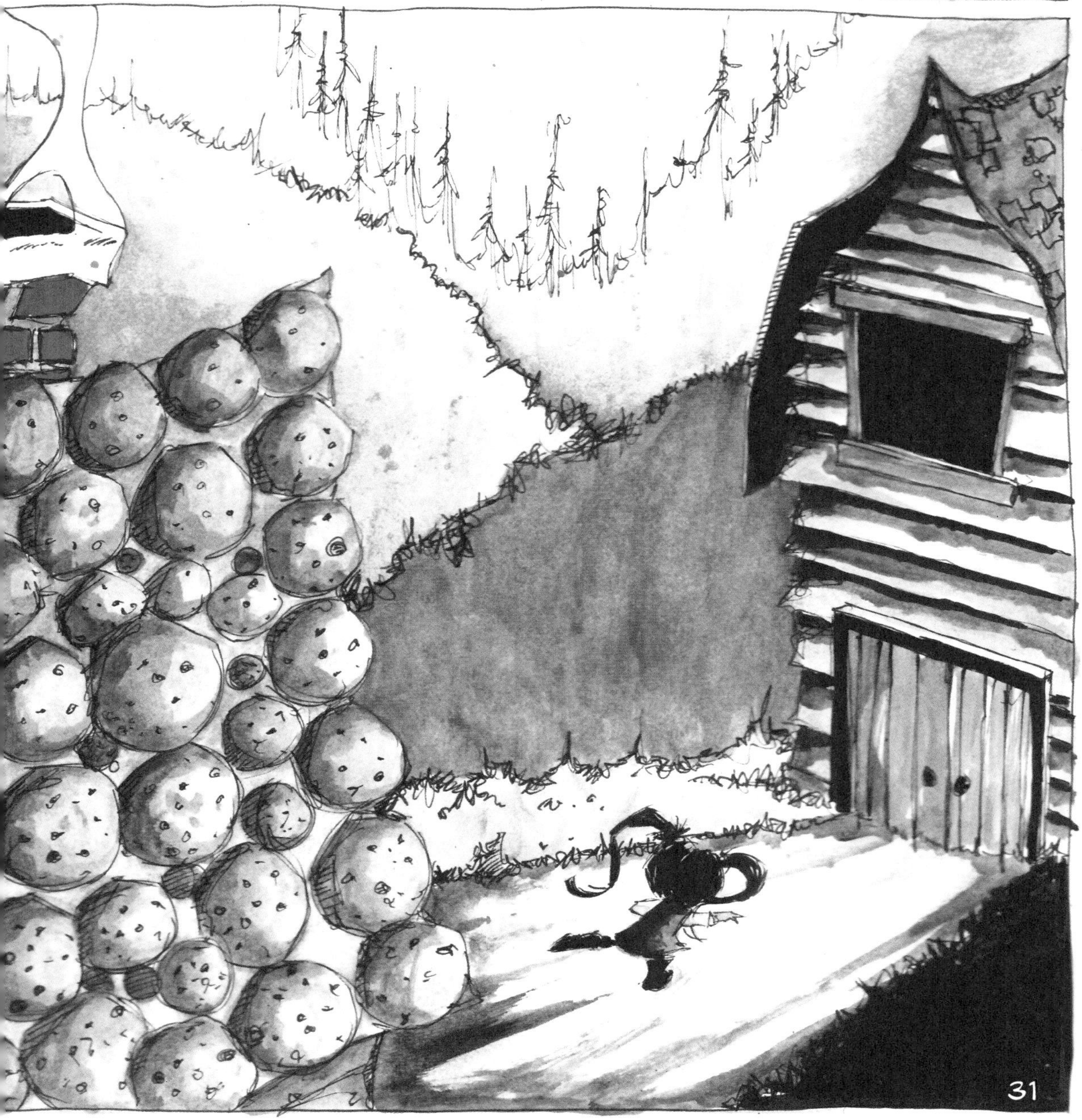

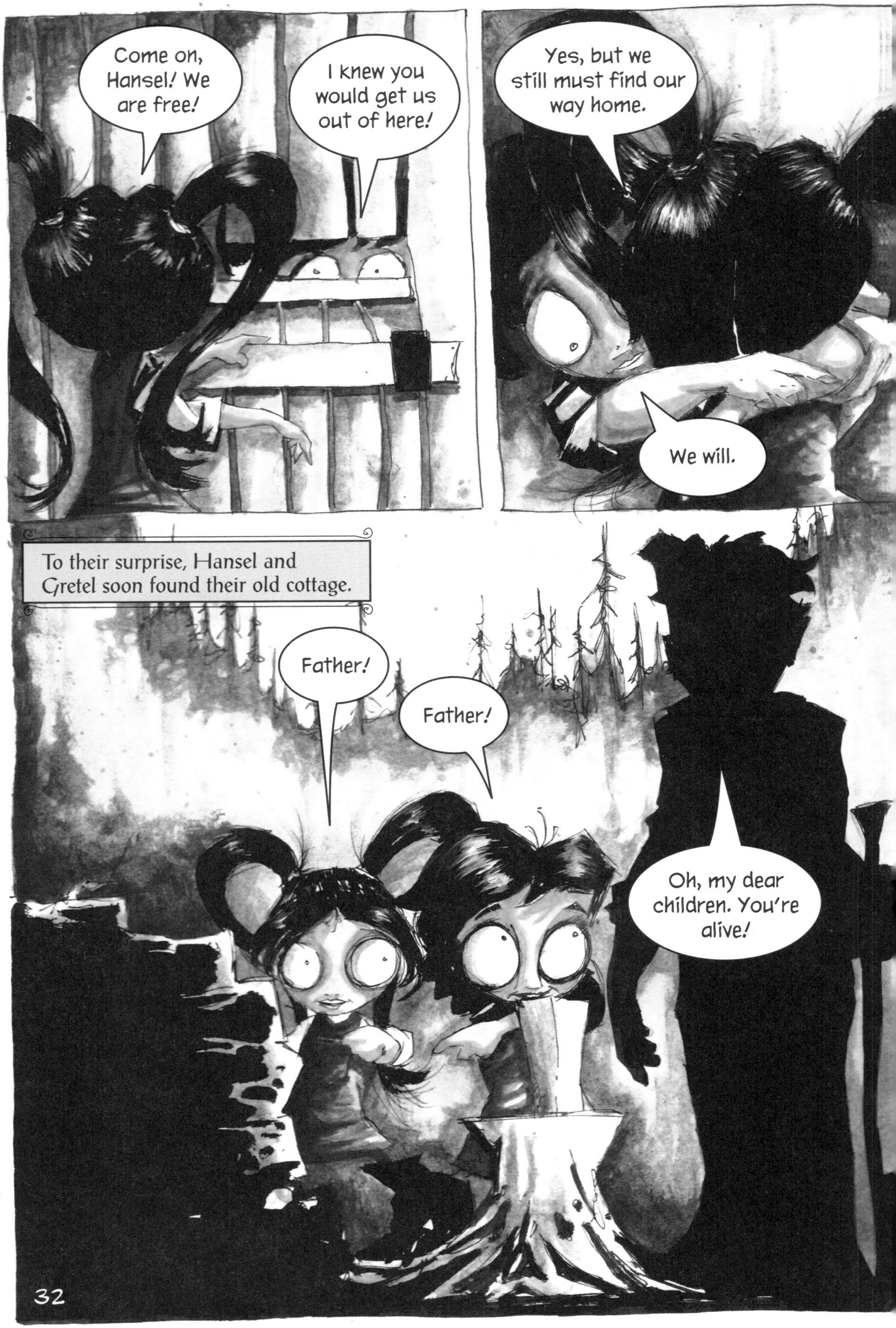
Come on, Hansel! We are free!
I knew you would get us out of here!
Yes, but we still must find our way home.
We will.
To their surprise, Hansel and Gretel soon found their old cottage.
Father!
Father!
Oh, my dear children. You're alive!

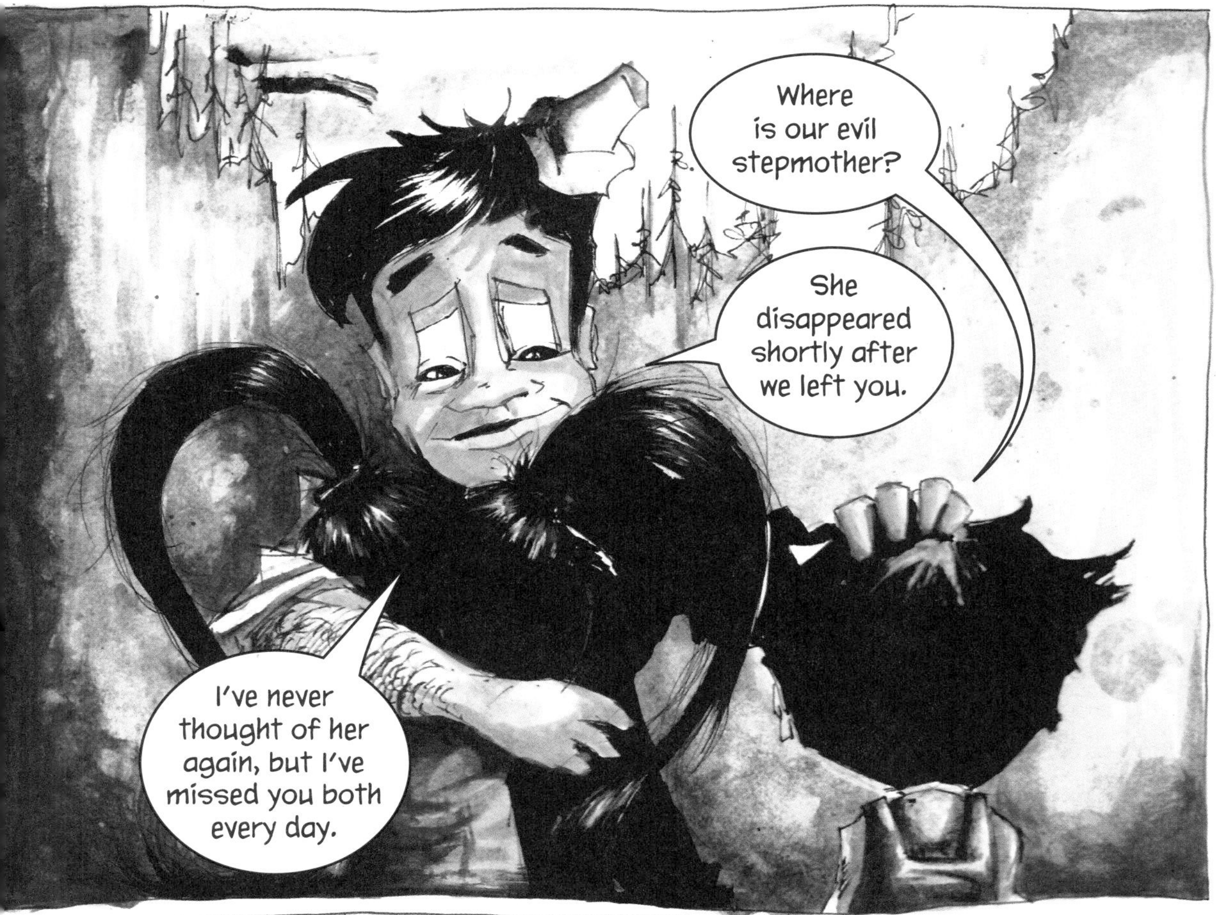
Where is our evil stepmother?
She disappeared shortly after we left you.
I've never thought of her again, but I've missed you both every day.

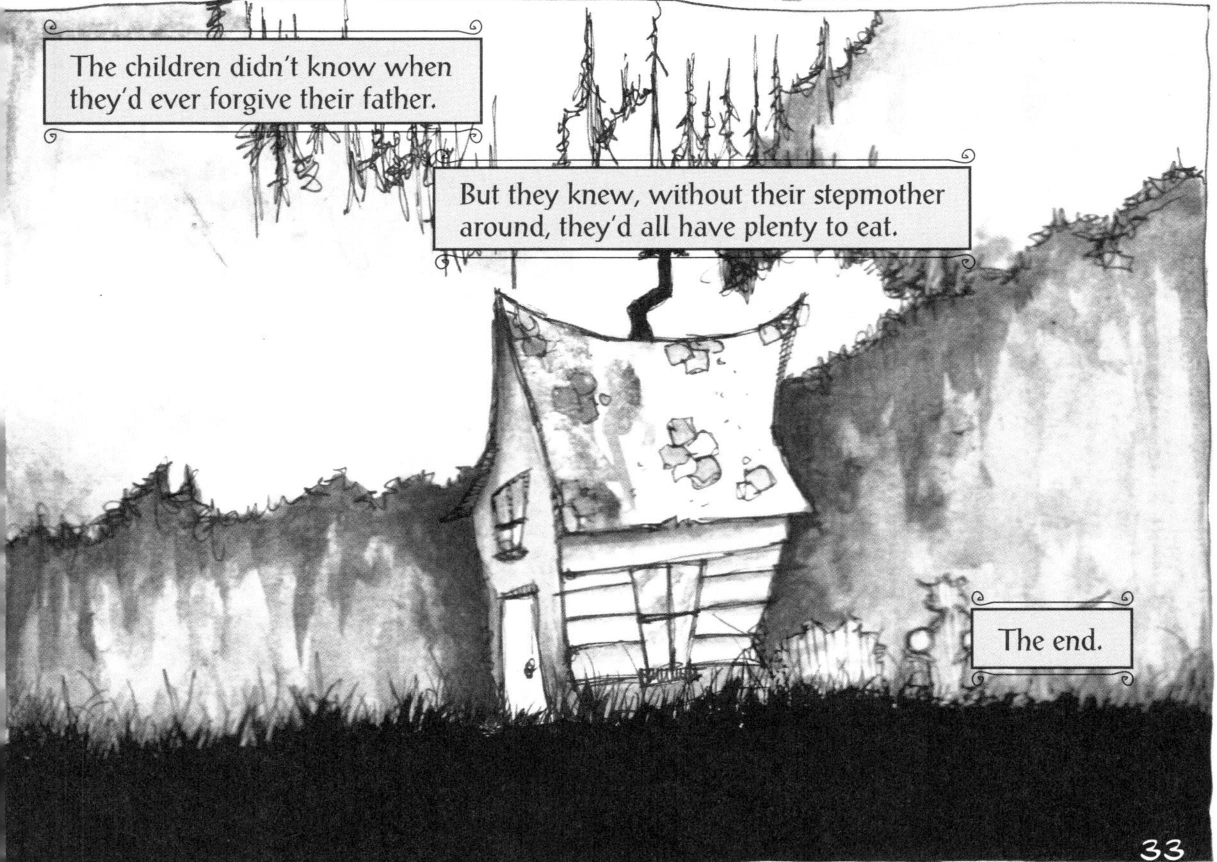
The children didn't know when they'd ever forgive their father.
But they knew, without their stepmother around, they'd all have plenty to eat.
The end.

About the Author

Growing up in a small Minnesota town, Donald Lemke kept himself busy reading anything from comic books to classic novels. Today, Lemke works as a children's book editor and pursues a master's degree in publishing from Hamline University in St. Paul, Minnesota. Lemke has written a variety of children's books and graphic novels. His ideas often come to him while running along the inspiring trails near his home.

About the Illustrator

Sean Dietrich was born in Baltimore, Maryland, and now lives in San Diego, California. He's been drawing since the age of 4. He had his first art show at the age of 6, self published his first comic book at 16, and has won more than 50 art awards throughout the years. When he's not drawing, Dietrich says he spends too much time in front of the TV playing video games.

Glossary

cottage (KOT-ij)—a small house

fattening (FAT-ten-ing)—feeding someone extra food to make him or her plump or fat

groveling (GROV-uhl-ing)—being unnaturally friendly or polite to someone

ma'am (MAM)—a formal title for a woman

nibble (NIB-uhl)—to take small, gentle bites of something

plump (PLUHMP)—somewhat fat or round in shape

shutters (SHUHT-urz)—movable window covers that help keep light out of a building

stable (STAY-buhl)—a building where horses or cattle are kept

stepmother (STEP-muhth-ur)—a woman who married a person's father that is not the person's birth mother

stew (STOO)—a dish made of meat or fish and vegetables cooked slowly in water

woodcutter (WOOD-kuht-ur)—someone who cuts down trees for firewood

The History of Hansel and Gretel

Like most fairy tales, the story of Hansel and Gretel is based on a long oral tradition. People in Europe and other places around the world often told stories of two children left in a dangerous forest. For hundreds of years, these imaginitive tales were passed from person to person and never written down.

In the early 1800s, brothers Jacob and Wilhelm Grimm started collecting many of these folktales. The Grimm brothers heard several of today's most famous stories including "Cinderella," "Snow White," and "Rapunzel." Scholars believe a woman named Henriette Dorothea Wild first told the Grimm brothers the story of Hansel and Gretel. They believe she heard the tale in the town of Cassel, Germany. In 1812, Jacob and Wilhelm Grimm published their book of collected stories called *Children's and Household Tales*.

Early versions of the Hansel and Gretel story were slightly different than today. The original story called the two children simply Little Brother and Little Sister. The Grimm brothers chose the names Hansel and Gretel. These were some of the most popular German names at the time.

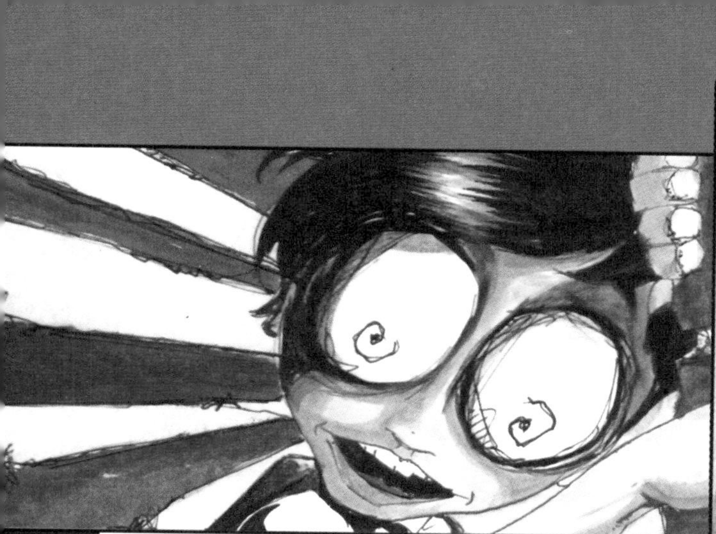

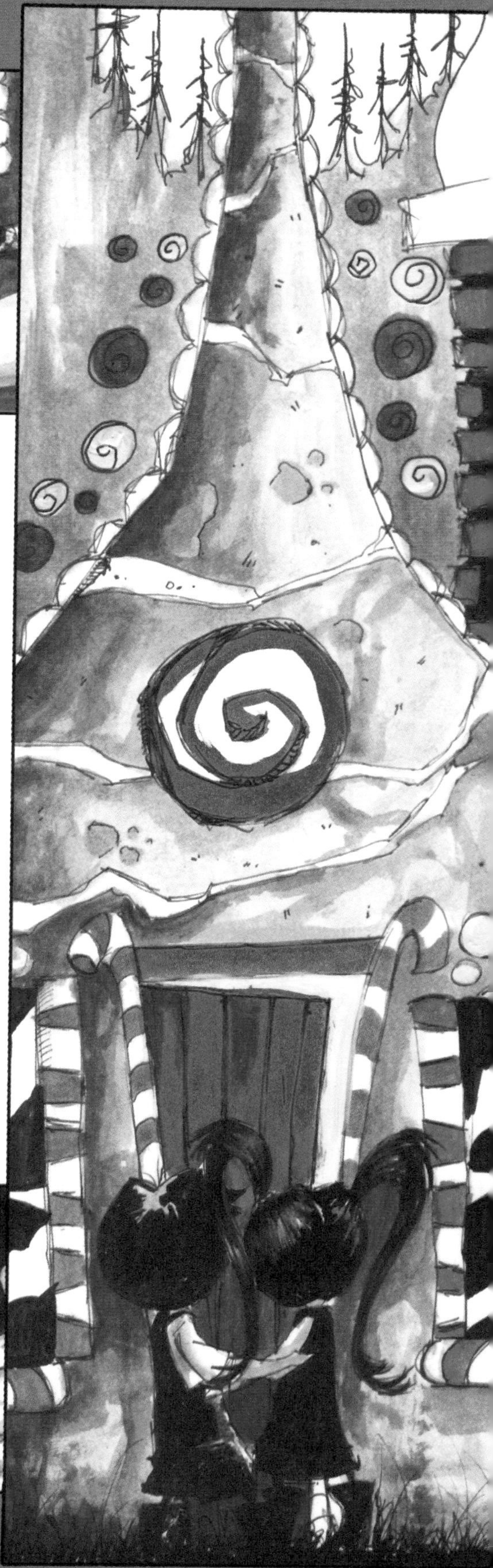

Also in the original Hansel and Gretel fairy tale, the stepmother was the children's real mother. Jacob and Wilhelm Grimm decided an evil stepmother would be less likely to scare childhood readers.

Today, the Grimms' book of stories is known as *Grimm's Fairy Tales*. The book is still read by people around the world and has been translated into more than 160 different languages.

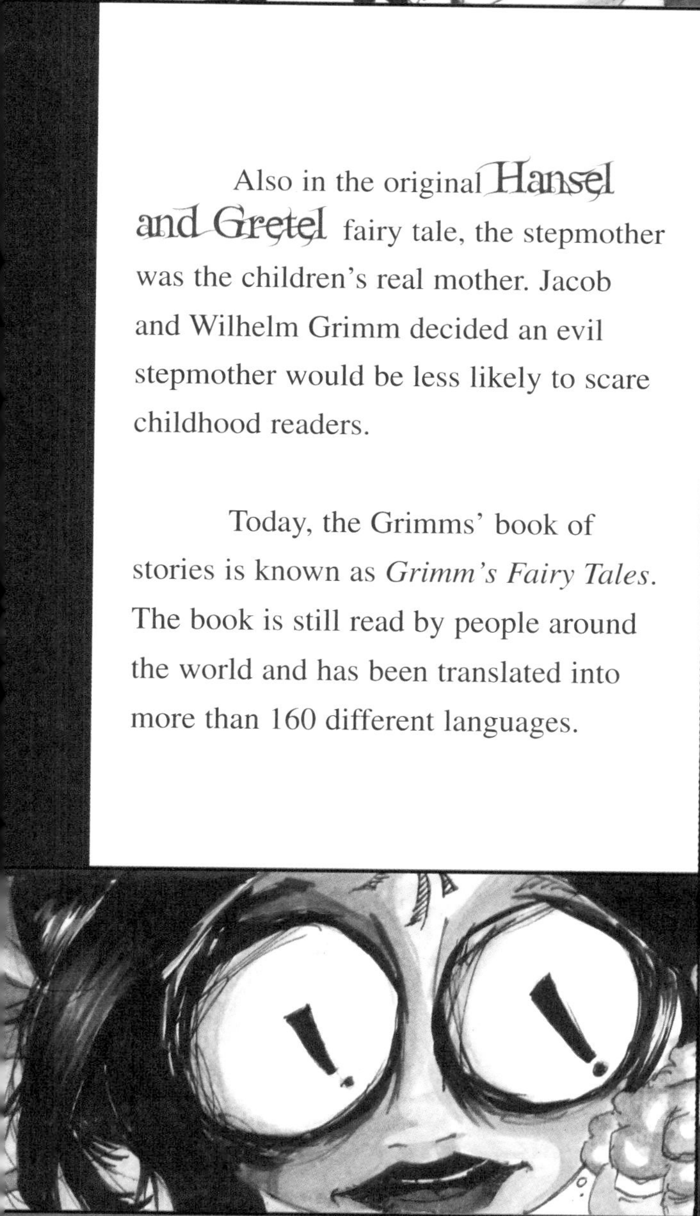

Discussion Questions

1. Why do you think the mean old lady's house was made of candy?

2. Hansel and Gretel's father left them in the forest. Do you think they should ever forgive him?

3. In some Hansel and Gretel stories, the stepmother turns out to be the mean old lady. Do you think the stepmother in this story could have also been the lady in the candy house? Why or why not?

Writing Prompts

1. Fairy tales are fantasy stories, often about wizards, goblins, giants, and fairies. Many fairy tales have a happy ending. Write your own fairy tale. Then, read it to a friend or family member.

2. Imagine you could build a house out of your favorite foods. Would your house have spaghetti carpet? How about cookies for doorknobs? Describe what your food house would look like.

3. Pretend you are the author and write a second part to the Hansel and Gretel story. Will Hansel and Gretel ever see their stepmother again? Will they forgive their father? You decide.

Internet Sites

The book may be over, but the adventure is just beginning.

Do you want to read more about the subjects or ideas in this book? Want to play cool games or watch videos about the authors who write these books? Then go to FactHound. At *www.facthound.com*, you'll be able to do all that, and more. The FactHound website can also send you to other safe Internet sites.

Check it out!

Edison Twp. Public Library
Clara Barton Branch
141 Hoover Ave.
Edison N.J. 08837

12/08

EDISON TWP. FREE PUBLIC LIBRARY

3 9360 00646660 4